Marvelous Secrets

"*Marvelous Secrets* is a marvelous read. You'll want to get comfortable first—take the phone off the hook, get a glass of iced tea, put your feet up . . . and savor these well-written, good-hearted stories which reflect Marian Coe's own wisdom and lively sense of adventure."

>**Lee Smith,** author of celebrated novels and story collections including *Oral History,* . . . *Fair and Tender Ladies,* and *News of the Spirit.*

"In this story collection, novelist Marian Coe serves us a sumptuous feast of stories to feed the soul."

>**Dr. Allen Speer,** professor at Lees-McRae College and author of *Voices from Cemetery Hill.*

"*Marvelous Secrets* gives us a voice full of grace and wisdom. Like all good story writers, Marian Coe is a connoisseur of life and shares this with Southern charm and wit and a sense of wonder. These stories are fresh and insightful and each one speaks to us about the complexity of simple lives."

>**Gail Adams,** author of *The Purchase of Order,* a Flannery O'Conner Award winner, and teacher of creative writing at the University of West Virginia.

"There are no strident pages in Marian Coe's stories, none overblown or overwrought. But there is a wonderful variety of subtle tones, sometimes wry, sometimes dismayed, sometimes foreboding—but always openhearted. The title story speaks of a lamp that glows yellow warm on a stack of books. That is the same kind of friendly and inviting light that *Marvelous Secrets* gives off. It is a comfort to have and to keep."

>**Fred Chappell,** novelist and Poet Laureate of North Carolina

Marvelous Secrets

Marian Coe

Manufactured in the United States of America

Copyright © 2000 Marian Coe

All rights reserved; no part of this publication may be reproduced, stored in a retrieval system, or transmitted, in any form or by any means, electronic, mechanical, photocopying, recording, or otherwise, without the prior written permission of the author.
This is a work of fiction. Names, characters, and incidents are the product of the author's imagination. Any resemblance to actual events or persons, living or dead, is entirely coincidental.

Publisher's Catalog-in-Publication
(Provided by Quality Books, Inc.)

Coe, Marian.
    Marvelous secrets / Marian Coe. -- 1st ed.
    p. cm.
    ISBN: 0-9633341-8-2

    I. Title.

PS3553.O345M37 2000   813'.6
                                             QBI00-278

Cover by John Cole, Graphic Designer
Interior design and typography by Publishing Professionals, New Port Richey, Florida

SouthLore Press
P.O. Box 847
Banner Elk, NC 28604

Local Color

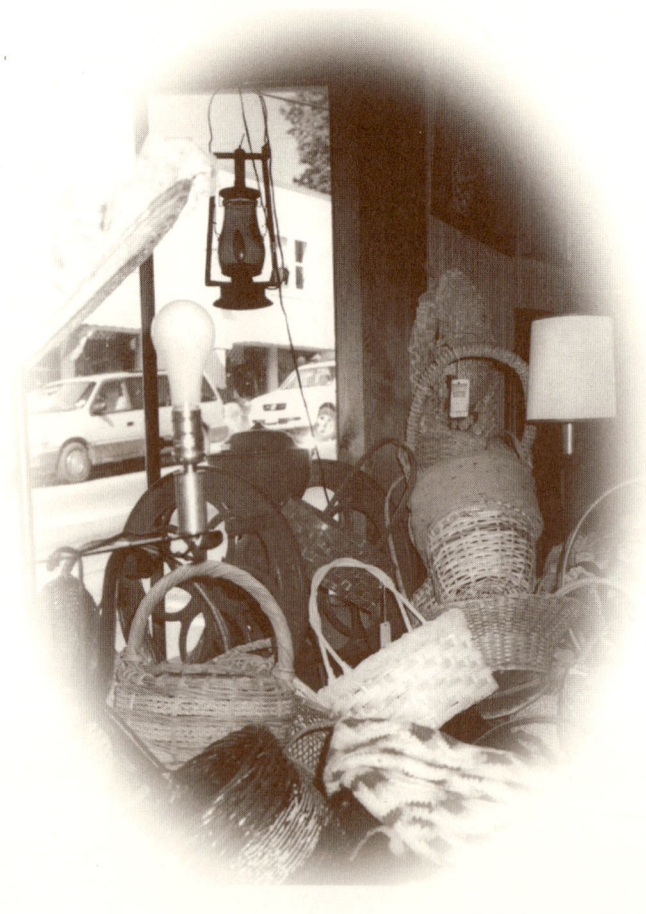

Local Color

To our summer people who tell me they enjoy getting this newsletter from Green Mountain Gap:

    Come on up now if you want to see spring happening. March can still blow in a snowy night but the pines are waking up and the hardwoods budding. Sheriff Milsap has checked the roads on the slopes around your houses. Says no signs of anybody messing around this winter, except a grouse must have hit one window hard. Don't worry, Eddie Milsap boarded it up and let those folks know.
    He cruises up there, regular. You might want to remember that when the police and fire departments have their Pig-Picking Benefit Barbecue in July. The same fellow who does Elvis Presley will be there again, if his tapes hold out. He looks like Elvis would look about now.
    The Laurel Inn opens in two weeks. Old man Taggart has been out there on the porch, giving the front rockers their annual coat of white enamel. Paint must be half an inch thick by now.

I don't like to pass on bad news but I'd best warn you, the town square is in danger of being purely ruined. No, this isn't about the highway streaking though town.

I know we've done our complaining about that. We still don't like that state road racing by high enough and close enough to give traffic the tacky backside view of the furniture store and firehouse and auto parts garage.

We've come to live with that. Some of the die-hards against the Blamed Highway have taken to McDonalds' egg sandwich breakfasts, but the Tylers at Home Cafe stay busy enough dishing out sawmill gravy and biscuits. Eggs you get there are from their own hens. I'll admit I see plenty of our folks in the new K-Mart down aways on the highway.

No, this is about the square itself and you know it's the heart of Green Mountain Gap even if the town is spreading out since all of your view houses went up on the slopes and the highway came through. Why, some of you in my shop have said the square is old and original enough to be on the National Registry same as the Laurel Inn.

Well, here's the thing. The old McKinney drugstore, boarded up for six years, has to come down. That's overdue. Trouble is, the McKinney corner is next to Luther Holloway's Hardware and poor Luther is being badgered to sell out. That hardware store is an original mountain business. Wilbur Spivey is doing the badgering.

Spivey is that little real estate fellow you might have seen prancing around town like a cocky proud Bantam rooster, gussied up, wearing a Stetson and smoking a cigar. He wants to sell three hundred foot of frontage to the Cozy Cabin people. They want to come in and put up a lot of their models which would turn the square into nothing but their display using the bank and the library and Laurel Inn as their backdrop.

You might wonder why a local real estate fellow would be willing to tacky up and sell out the square. Well, Spivey has been here only thirty years and besides, he's a trading fool, and trying to beat out Will Baines who still has some frontage after the state built the Blamed Highway on Baines land.

You'd think Luther Holloway would just tell Wilbur Spivey he doesn't want to sell, but no. Luther is a sweet old fellow, third generation behind that counter, but not good at speaking up for himself to outsiders or pushy folks or his wife. I'm not a gossip so I won't go into it here in the newsletter about his troubles at home.

I shouldn't close without letting you know I'm not one to sit back and complain. My Mama used to say, whiney folks blame problems on circumstances or God, but the Almighty expects us to use some gumption to change the circumstances. So I don't intend to sit back and let the square get ruined. Can't tell you how because right now I don't know. By the time you come in for summer, you'll see whatever happened.

        Yours truly,
        Sally Riddle at
        Saved Treasures Shop
        On The Square
        in Green Mountain Gap, NC
      With thanks to Mabel Hackett at the PO for running off these letters on the copy machine.

I'm leaning in the window, hanging up a patchwork quilt when I see Wilbur Spivey heading this way like a pesky rain cloud on my sunny day.

I keep on fiddling with the quilt, watching him strut along. Going into Luther's hardware to pester the poor man. Poor Luther has enough trouble right now at home. Sarah is riled up about that pregnant hippie girl who's been living in the back of the store.

I keep advising Luther: "You've told him, and I've told him, we're not going to sell out. No matter what. So be busy or somewhere else when he comes in."

Luther must have taken my advice and slipped out to the barber shop or cafe, because here comes Spivey out of the store and trotting this way. I back out of my window. Get busy dusting china by the time the door tinkles.

In he walks, beaming. "Morning, Miz Sally." He knows now to get rid of his cigar outside. Sets himself down in one of the rockers that I keep up front for company or tired tourists, parks his Stetson on his knee, and looks up at me with his pink beaming face.

"Percolator still hot back there? Don't mind if I have a cup, and I can save you from throwing out any biscuits."

"I never have to throw out any biscuits I bring in here, Wilbur Spivey. Someday when I stretch out this shop to my fifty feet between me and Luther, I'll put in four tables and serve lunch."

"Miz Sally, it's forty feet, and you don't make enough selling this old stuff to put yourself in the food business."

I look him right in the eye. "Four little tables." That high bald dome of his, with his little frame, reminds me of a shrewd old baby, glasses on the nose.

"My women customers will be glad to sit down for tea and chicken salad and hot rolls. Resting from their shopping," I tell him.

The door tinkles again and in come three now, oohing and ahhing like visitors do, minute they see all the quilts and china and lamps and old kitchen stuff filling this place. I say, "Make yourselves to home ladies. There's two more rooms in the back."

Spivey watches them mince on back there. "They gonna buy anything?"

"They hafta look." Spivey knows the square gets customers not only from our own slopes, but from Elk River, Grandfather Mountain. Linville Ridge, Hound Ears, all those manicured mountains around these parts with fancy gates.

But I make my point just the same. "If their husbands aren't off playing golf, they'll be spending time looking around in Luther's hardware."

"Lookers. But do they buy? Miz Sally, what they come looking for is *local color*— that's what they call it. The Inn's dining room, Luther's gee-gaws, and all the old timey stuff you have in here —it's all local color for their *a-muse-ment*."

"And why do you reckon, Wilbur Spivey? The way the world's going, trying to keep up with the TV commercials and scare movies,

7

people need to see this kind of place once in a while. One that stays real as the mountains."

"You're a sentimental woman and stubborn to boot. I'd think an able-bodied, unfettered widow like you would be smart enough to let me unload this old shop for you. You could move down to Florida and find a rich old coot who happens to like stubborn women who can cook. I'll take cream and sugar, and butter, case you've forgotten."

I could tell Spivey what he calls sentimental means having mellow feelings about somebody or something besides pride in yourself, only I don't expect him to listen. I go back and check on the ladies who are sighing over a china pattern their grandmothers used. They make a fuss when they see me taking biscuits out of an old cooker where I keep them warm.

"Oh, I bring in hot biscuits ever morning and hand them out, long as they last, to be neighborly. Same reason I have rockers up front. Those quilts you're looking at? I do them all winter."

I set up a tray for Spivey, a mug of coffee, two biscuits, dab of butter, a pitcher of milk out of my little fridge, and bring it up front, set it on a needlepoint stool in front of the old buzzard.

"Mighty fine, Miz Sally." He starts buttering a biscuit and gives me a sneaky smile. "Know who was behind the counter at Luther's?"

"Young Josh McKinney, needing something to do, waiting around until you find the right person to buy his granddaddy's old corner. I'll be glad to see that old eye-sore torn down. But we don't want any new ones to go up."

He taps a stubby finger against his cup, eyebrows going up and down. "That hippie girl is still in there behind the counter. In her condition, mind you. What do you know about that?"

I don't blink. "I already told you what I know. That Cassie is a sweet little thing. You know she wanted to stay on when her friends got run out from the creek campgrounds last November. She doesn't have a husband and she's going to have a baby any time now. So?"

"Mighty foolish of Luther to harbor that girl. Folks are talking. Talk's getting back to Sarah."

"Oh for goodness sakes, Wilbur Spivey, you know Sarah Holloway fed Cassie all winter. Accepted that as her Christian duty."

Back in November, when the other hippies left, and Cassie stayed, Luther had told me his own reason for giving her a place to stay. "You can't push a nesting bird off the nest until her time."

"Just telling you a fact, Miz Sally. Luther's pulling his head in and closing his ears about what folks are saying, letting that girl work there. Miz Holloway gets testy about her good name."

I hold my tongue and watch him butter the second biscuit.

"Now Miz Sally, let's be practical. Luther needs to sell out. He's holding on to that old store like life itself. He's no spring chicken. Needs capital bad. His stock's way down. Got no son to take over. Big stores coming in ever'where near here. Best thing Luther can do is sell that store while these folks are here with money. He could give the wife a new house better than that old place out there by their tobacco field."

Lord, most of that is true. I watch him pop on his Stetson and prance out. I take the tray back, trying not to imagine half the square turning into a Cozy Cabin parking lot, jam up next to me, and Luther stuck at home like a lost soul in front of the TV. Have to make myself smile as the women trail out, gushing about the shop, not buying a thing.

The door tinkles and it's a relief to see it's Josh McKinney. He drops in the chair Spivey left, shakes his head at coffee, stretches his long legs and groans. "Spivey been busting you too, Sally?"

I take the other rocker, glad for real company. I watched Josh grow up summers when he was a red-headed skinny kid, no more than twelve or thirteen, working in his granddaddy McKinney's drug store. Now he's a sober twenty-four with problems on his mind, I can tell.

"Sally, I hate this push for all of you to sell out, but Granddad's property needs a bulldozer and I need the money."

"I know that, Josh."

"I'm waiting around to make sure some deal goes through. Not that I'm in a hurry to get back to Atlanta."

"They holding your job?"

He grimaces. "I'm on borrowed time. But I hate to leave without knowing what's going to happen to Luther. And Cassie."

"That's a problem, I know."

"When I get the money from that corner, I may go back to school. Being back here I realize I hate my job—sitting in front of a computer all day. Do I sound like a first class jerk, complaining?

"Sounds more like honest confessions to me."

He grins like the kid I remember. "Going inside that old boarded up store really spooked me. The hardware store is even older—seventy-five years?—but it's still live and working. I get a real charge from that place. Those oiled wood floors. Nooks and crannies. Luther can reach in a box and pull out any single screw a customer needs. Or asks about."

I nod, thinking of those summer folks poking around over there. Looking at *local color*, I guess. Maybe not spending much.

Josh rocks a minute, glancing around, smiling at all my stuff. "You're both something, you and Luther. You should charge admission. Imagine a hardware store today that has a hog scraper. But truth is, Luther needs to get in some new stock. He doesn't like to talk about money. Doesn't know the first thing about advertising. If he's going to stay in business, he'd better begin. Plenty of building going on in the county. All Luther does is tend store. And Sarah is really on his case."

"Lord help us, I know."

We're quiet a minute before Josh goes on.

"I'd forgotten there were real folks like you and Luther. No offense. This whole town is an anachronism, with characters like Spivey."

I let that pass because he sounded so wistful saying it.

"And I'd forgotten there were females like Cassie—gutsy, honest and yet still sweet-natured as a kitten. She likes it here, doesn't let the old biddies get to her."

"Town's old," I agree, "like a piece of china, a one of a kind pattern, chipped but still genuine, so it's valuable, mind you. That's why I'm not about to let anybody ruin the square if I can help it."

Josh wags his head in sympathy.

"I'd better get back. Cassie needs help. She shouldn't be picking up anything heavy. Or having to deal with folks with righteous faces as if they're looking at a fallen woman. You know, she's learning the stock over there. I am too. Luther keeps ducking out, hiding from Spivey."

"I hear Sarah is all stirred up."

Josh gives me a weary grin. "Spivey talked to the preacher who went out and told Sarah it wasn't Christian charity to let Luther keep that girl in his store, it was condoning unwed motherhood. Doesn't that frost you? Sally, you know Cassie. She is the nicest thing that's ever happened to Luther since they lost the son in Vietnam. Would you believe Cassie has him listening to her read Whitman and Keats? He says he never knew there were such 'purty' words."

"I know. She comes over here and wanders through, with a dreaming face looking at everything. Like a woman wanting to line her nest. Only thing she's bought is an old poetry book and baby quilt."

"It really bothers me, what's going to happen to them." Josh gets up stretching his lanky frame, frowning. "I can't leave here not knowing. Her time is coming up."

"Her time and the square," I admit. "My own place is just big enough for one old lady and a cat."

"Who's old? Not you, Sally." He stands there thinking. "Maybe I can sell Spivey on finding another buyer for my corner, so he won't be all fired determined to get the Cozy Cottage folks in."

"You don't sell Wilbur Spivey anything. He has to think he's buying it away from you."

"I'd better get back over and help Cassie," Josh says.

By noon, two women come in, a couple of tall sisters, chatty and looking around, telling me they've just retired from some big store in Chicago. They're in town for their Aunt Katherine's funeral. Takes me a minute to realize they mean old Katie Hartley, the one with all the cats, who died this week. The sisters are looking for a realtor to sell her place, a beat down old house on a pretty meadow of twenty acres, six miles out of town on the county road.

I start to send them to Miss Donnelly who's handles farm property when she has a mind to. But I think, maybe a house deal could keep Spivey busy and off our backs. I call him up, nice as you please, and tell him I'm sending the sisters over.

Next day, I'm opening up when in walk a couple of fellows who turn out to be Cozy Cabin people. They buy a lot of genuine country stuff for some of their models they have in other places around these mountains. Not bad fellows, really.

They say they don't blame me for wanting to hold on to the looks of the square, but their presence is going to be good for some little town, once they come in. People coming to look at the models would be sure to shop in my place.

I don't argue. Just sit them down for some coffee and hot biscuits. I must admit I enjoy dealing too. I ask why they don't want to put their models up on the highway. Told them where they'd find Will Baines, but they shook their heads. They'd already checked that out. Didn't like that frontage up against the mountain cut out to a red bank.

Then I think of Miss Katie's place. Tell them about that. "You'll find Wilbur Spivey out there now." I go on about how pretty Miss Katie's place is, a rolling meadow right off from a county road, mountain slopes rising in the back.

When they go out, I sit down to worry about what I've done. Have I run off some real customers? How do I know for sure Luther isn't ready to give up and take the Cozy Cabin money? And there's Josh, needing somebody to buy that old eyesore corner.

Two mornings later, Luther jangles my front door, sticks his head in, more excited than I've ever seen the man. "Miz Sally, we've got us a baby girl."

It takes a minute to get the story. Middle of the night, Josh took Cassie down to the hospital, stayed there pacing like a daddy. This morning, as Luther opened the store, Josh called with the news. Told Luther to get Sarah and come down.

"Don't know if she'll go," Luther tells me, standing in the door, worried now.

"You tell Sarah you two have to go. And make sure she holds the baby. Ask the nurse. They'll let her."

That Sarah is not a mean woman, just bottled up inside. Maybe she's never gotten over losing her only boy in Vietnam. I'm counting on her holding that baby.

I'm cleaning my front window when I see Wilbur Spivey heading my way, face still splotchy from Katie

Hartley's cats. Poor man is allergic. He is prancing along, like his old foxy self, because he has made commission on Josh's corner as well as Miss Katie's property.

"Miz Sally, I got a bargain for you," he says, not bothering to take a rocker. "I'm selling all of Katie's furniture to the Antiques store. But that woman's bureau drawers and closets are stuffed full and have to be cleaned out. I'll sell you the whole mess for a hundred bucks. Must be some old stuff in there you can sell. But you'd have to go in and get it out. I paid a fellow to haul those cats to the shelter, but I'm not going back in that place."

"What kind of a deal is that, Wilbur Spivey? I'll go in and clear out the drawers—for sixty."

"Seventy-five and it's yours."

"Sixty if I have to go in and clean it out."

"You're a stubborn woman, Miz Sally. Go get the stuff. For sixty." He trots on out.

I knew old Katie Bailey. Knew she was a real dresser twenty years ago when she first moved back here. Knew she'd been a pack rat since. I figure it will take three days to load up what she has in there.

Today, Josh walks in looking the happiest I've ever seen the boy. He's even brought me a picture of Sara-Joy. I'm so worn out from what I found at Katie's all I can do is rest and rock.

He sits there on the edge of his seat, grinning at me, letting me fuss about what's on my mind.

"It took two bottles of cold water soap and a night of ironing and mending," I tell him, "but I do have some of the finest old costumey dresses and hats that ever hung in a closet. Besides her boxes of jewelry, stuff from the Twenties on to the Forties."

Josh hops up, wanting to see. He acts like a kid at Christmas when I show him the lot, piled up in back.

"You've got a windfall here, Sally. Vintage clothing is romantic one-of-a-kind stuff that sells. This beaded dress alone should go for seventy-five bucks, maybe more. You've out-traded the old trader Spivey."

"I wouldn't claim that. Before I closed up last night, he came in here to boast. He's selling the Cozy Cottage people a thousand acres—Katie's meadow and the slopes behind it. They're going to develop the mountain up there. Hate to see it. The Blamed Highway filling up and now the county road. They'll have to widen that too."

Josh did a slow whistle. "Customers, Sally, customers. Price we have to pay. Now you sit still and listen to my news."

May 15

Since I may have worried you summer neighbors with my last letter, I'm not waiting until you get here in June to report what's happening. Yes, you'll find changes going on this summer. For one thing, a lot of messy road construction. And a new store is going up on the square, on that old McKinney corner next to Luther's hardware.

Josh McKinney, a young man from Atlanta, is buying half interest in Luther Holloway's Town Hardware. Josh is going to stay in Green Mountain Gap and run it with Luther—advertise and bring in hiking boots and sweaters and such, like the Mast Store in Boone. Two sisters who came to sell off their aunt's land plan to put up a new building on that McKinney corner. Going to put in a gift shop. The two ladies are retired from the business, so I guess they know what they're doing.

Oh yes, Josh McKinney is getting married tomorrow to a young lady named Cassie Jenner who has been working in the hardware store. Both are college people who love these mountains more than big cities and computer jobs.

I don't know who looks happier. Josh will be inheriting a baby daughter—Sara-Joy—with the wedding. She's named after Luther's wife, Sarah, who is taking over like a grandma. Changed that woman all around, that baby. Josh will be building a house next to what used to be the Holloway's tobacco field.

Yes, the Cozy Cabin people will be on the square, with a little information office where the shoe store is moving out. Those folks going to work at the K-Mart.

With all this happening, I'm extending my building forty feet up against the hardware store. I gave up the idea of a little tea shop. Need the space for all the old-new clothes I've brought in. You'll see, once you're back for summer. Already the jonquils are up and rhododendron blooming.

Yours truly,
Sally Riddle of
Saved Treasures Shop
On The Square

Marian Coe

All The Time There Is

All The Time There Is

With the morning desert alive and silent around them, they stack luggage in the rented car and drive out of Ghost Ranch, heading for Albuquerque and the flight back to Charlotte.

"We could have stayed a few more hours," she murmurs as they turn onto the ribbon of highway. "We could have walked after breakfast. There's a place, imagine, where dinosaur bones have been found."

Already her husband is intent on the road ahead that streaks through the pinon-dotted landscape. "Not enough time," he says. "It's an hour back to Santa Fe and another into Albuquerque. With the car to turn in."

"We've never missed a flight."

"Because we believe in getting to a check-in desk an hour ahead."

Again she sighs. "They look timeless out there."

"Sagebrush? Crazy rocks?"

"The mountains on the horizon. They stay rooted no matter how fast we go."

The car speeds along under pale, open sky. Far ahead, a single vehicle becomes a battered slow-moving truck. As they approach to pass, two Indian children wave from the back.

She glances at her husband's intent profile. "You have that look. Your mind's already back in the office. I meant to forget mine. Maybe a week isn't long enough to really let go."

They fall silent in the humming car until a weathered sign ahead has her sitting upright, instantly eager. "Oh, look, Jake! Coming up, that must be the old Spanish restaurant they told us about. Let's stop. Please."

Grimacing, he says, "We were going to grab a bite at the airport, remember."

"Look, it *is* the Rancho de Chimyo."

"Megan—" He sees her exuberance, gives a reluctant smile and slows the car. "Okay. We take a look, have some coffee and get going."

A rubble drive leads off the highway up to a higher level where the long squat restaurant sits behind dusty bushes against the solemn grandeur of open desert.

"Sure you want to take time for this?" he asks, but they're out of the car now and the sharp wind sends them hurrying toward the place.

The small foyer's greeting is a muted Spanish beat from an unseen source and a stone fountain of trickling water framed by red paper flowers. Looking down from above the fountain is the peacefully benign face of a ceramic Virgin Mary.

Megan leads the way into the darker restaurant, a long room of timbered ceilings, tables, and underfoot, dark red Spanish tiles. Behind a massive mahogany bar, a lone attendant nods a welcome and continues to polish a glass with an unhurried rhythm.

"Must not be open, no one's here," Jake mutters at the darkened, empty tables. Megan grabs his arm. "Down there, by the fire," she says.

At the far end of the room, logs glow on a huge stone hearth, silhouetting a seated couple. They head toward the warmth, pausing at the adjacent table to ask, "Mind if we if share the fire?"

"Oh, my dears, join us, of course," the woman says. "My husband and I are celebrating." The petite turned-up face seems flushed by some special pleasure.

Megan loves to watch people. And here is this neat little woman, twenty years or so older than herself, with a young girl look about her, in the funny knit hat, embroidered blouse and denim skirt sweeping down to her small ankles under the table.

The lanky husband looks up, nodding. The tanned lined face and faded blue eyes remind Megan of Gary Cooper. And here he is, still romantic, reaching over to press his wife's hand like that. "This is Dura's favorite restaurant," he tells them with the soft drawl Megan expects. "We drove out here for this special day."

They settle at the next table, Megan beaming her silent delight at the glowing hearth, wood and pinon smells, faint beat of Spanish guitar and Jake looking relaxed for a change. Besides, they have this pair of old lovers to watch, celebrating life or whatever.

Introductions are exchanged. Megan and Jake from Charlotte, North Carolina; Dura and Link from Santa Fe.

"So what should we order?" Jake asks. "We do have a plane to catch. But this is a great place to find on a cold day in New Mexico."

Link describes Dura's favorite dishes as the dark-eyed server arrives, placing the steaming plates on their small round table. Chili rellenos and chicken enchilada and Spanish rice and something else with blue corn meal. "I am drinking Tecata with salt and lime, and I toast Dura here with her glass of Dos Equis."

Their own orders arrive, the server glides away, the logs settle down, lined with crimson embers and the pinon aroma. Gingerly pushing aside green chilies, Megan relishes her hot enchiladas, trying to catch Jake's eye. Is he watching their companion couple? They seem ageless, so intent they are on this moment, and each other, even neglecting their food for their murmured remarks. And now, turning to ask more than politely, almost eagerly, about their own visit.

"I took a whole week off to come out here for an art class at the Ghost Ranch," Jake says ruefully. "But yes, it was a good experience."

"He's wanted to do that for years but never has the time," Megan adds. "I took long walks and enjoyed the library there. It's the first vacation we've taken . . . oh, since forever, it seems. We're on our way home. Back to work."

"Did you walk out to Georgia O'Keefe's cottage near the ranch?" Dura asks, her fork idle, as if this is important to know. "That's one of my favorite places around Ghost Ranch."

"I did, two afternoons." Megan sips at her beer to cool her dancing taste buds. "Jake and I have fifteen more years at least before we can slow down and enjoy life as you seem to do. With no deadlines."

Because this older couple waits, like polite listeners, with unreadable smiles—self-satisfaction, amusement? —Megan adds quickly, "But what about you? Are you both native westerners? It's so different out here."

"Link is a writer," Dura answers with pride. "He was a studio writer for years, wrote the story for some of the movies you may remember. Westerns. Writers never got paid but once back then. Even if it turned out to be Shane."

Link smiles, nods, tells them a funny story about movie westerns. "And my wife here was one of the sweet faced females in bonnets who looked out of covered wagons. But you won't find our names on the credits if one of the oldies surface on your TV screen."

"So you're from North Carolina," Dura says, bright faced. "You have your own kind of mountains there, different from the Rockies. They must have their special beauty."

"That's the Blue Ridge part," Megan says. "We're in a city that keeps growing, like everywhere else."

"What's it like there?" Dura asks. "I never got that far east."

Jake tells them about the mountains and the Outer Banks, but adds, joking about a reality accepted, "We don't have time to get be the tourist, mountains or shore, with a new company going." Frowning at his wrist watch, "In fact—but this stop has been good. Truly a pleasure meeting you both."

He looks at Megan. "I'll take care of the check at the bar. I'll see you at the car."

Jake strides out. Megan gets up. Ready to say good-bye, she sees now their colorful plates, their avowed favorite dishes, are scarcely touched.

"You're not eating?" What has she missed here? Something. . .

Dura is looking at her husband, words softened to a whisper. "I'm sorry. I just can't." It sounds like an apology.

He reaches across the dishes, pressing her hand again. "It's all right."

Megan stands there, feeling the intruder who has made some terrible, crass mistake. When the husband looks up, the faded blue eyes are bright, the look direct. "This is Dura's first day out of the hospital. She's been there for awhile. We've been looking forward to coming back here to her favorite place."

"All this time . . . Jake and I have been talking about ourselves . . . and you."

"And we enjoyed the visit, didn't we?" Link says.

Dura looks up, the smile in place again. "Oh, yes, dear, a pleasure."

Megan sees now what the bright look means. Not ordinary self-satisfied pleasure. It's an eagerness, a willingness, to enjoy the present moment.

Megan has to ask. "And now?"

"We have five years before we know what else," the husband drawls. It sounds confident, as if talking about all the time in the world.

Megan tries to return their smiles, makes her fumbling good-bye. She heads out across the darkened restaurant, turns back once to see them there, the celebrating pair, outlined by firelight.

Outside cold wind nudges at her face like something alive. She climbs in the car beside Jake, closes her hand over his on the ignition key, and tells him what the Santa Fe couple were celebrating.

Back on the open highway, they ride for silent miles, watching the road ahead. It seems to stretch endlessly before them, like a gift.

Marian Coe

Marvelous Secrets

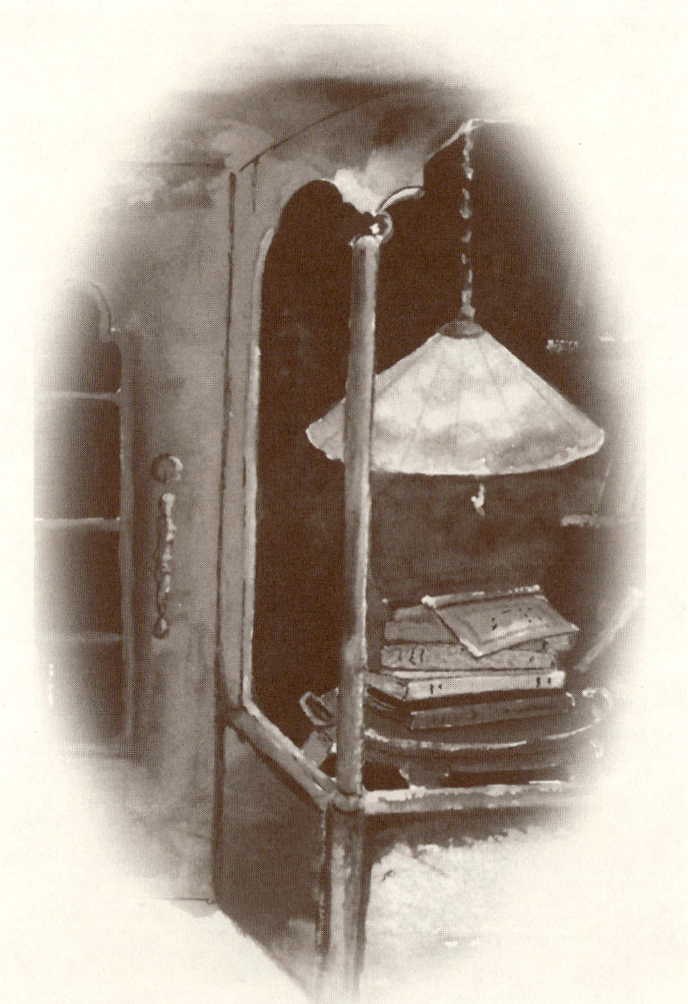

Marvelous Secrets

The old street of small shops—antiques, estate jewelry, and enigmas—intrigued me, so I was far from the hotel when the rain started. Why had I ignored those rumbling clouds? Now, a downpour. Which door to try for shelter?

In one window, a lamp glowed warm yellow on a stack of books. Old, once cherished kind of books.

I pushed open the door and plunged inside, into a narrow, deep shop, a virtual lamp-lit cave of books. Farther back, standing bookshelves made narrow corridors. Boston had an abundance of book stores, but none this cozy.

What ho—I'd made a lucky choice. The rainstorm pounding away outside was a muted reality here. Strains from a Spanish guitar came softly from its unseen source.

A woman emerged from the back, a tall, lithe person in a long dark sheath of a dress, single gold chain the only adornment; once-blonde hair pulled back from a clear brow, tied at the neck with a velvet ribbon.

"You're just in time," she greeted, sounding amused, but sympathetic.

Whatever she meant, I agreed. "I ignored those clouds until they caught me. I chose your door."

She smiled. "Chance and choice shape our lives—do you think? Make yourself comfortable. I'm making tea."

I sank in one of two deep chairs against the book wall and picked up the card on the low table in front. It read: *Marvelous Secrets. Owner, Pamela Wessner.*

Interesting woman, intriguing shop.

Strange, that remark she made about chance and choice—it happened to be the core issue I was attempting to address in a professional paper—what part chance happenings, what part conscious or subconscious choice—might determine what we choose to call, in retrospect, personal fate.

She returned with a tray, agreeing I wouldn't find a taxi in the deluge outside. I accepted one of the two delicate china cups of hot amber tea, said my thanks, sat back and sipped, looking around at rows of old leather spines as well as shiny ones, shadowed or glowing under lamp light.

"So you have walls of 'marvelous secrets'?"

"There for the finding." A pleasant, casual voice of a hostess, not a seller of whatever.

"I'm curious. I have to ask. You mentioned something—"

I told her about my paper in progress. Asked her opinion on that familiar question: which is the more causal in one's life—what happens outside of us and therefore to us, or the moves we choose to make?

She sat silent for a moment, looking into her tea, before placing the cup in its saucer. "My shelves offer a wealth of ideas, yes. Rather than browsing, or listening to my opinion—would you care to hear a story? It might offer some evidence."

So, in warm lamplight, rain droning outside, she told me this story about a woman she knew. A woman so stuck in a numbing life she didn't allow herself to know it, until it began to change. How? By chance or choice.

"You decide," my hostess said.

I settled back to listen. I remember it like this:

Marta Treadwell's days all began with the accepted sameness of a ticking clock. Or did, until a certain gray March day. By the evening—the ticking was more like a cuckoo clock, stuck on its hinges, chirping *wake-up*.

That morning, when the alarm droned at 6 o'clock, Marta turned it off and lay back, as usual, to allow herself minutes to accept the waiting realities. These included: Norton in the other twin bed, a solid lump, snoring, expecting breakfast in 45 minutes. It meant opening her eyes slowly, to check how fast the room was spinning. Pretty fast this morning. The two oak chests whipped past like squat wooden bulldogs, whirled by a silent wind.

Vertigo or not, she knew to put her feet flat on the floor, take in a breath and proceed with the morning's routine. Big robe pulled over the nightgown. In the bathroom, splash of water on the face, brush back the long skeins of hair, turning the color of smoke, carefully not looking too closely in the mirror.

Her age? Just beyond forty. No, she was not a reader of self-help books detailing the varieties of dissatisfaction one might overcome, or diet books promising ways to shed the thirty extra pounds accrued during the ten plus years she'd been married to, and cooking for, Norton. Nor did she dream of another life by reading paperback romances. Occasionally she leafed through old college books as if they were keepsakes from some other person's life. Mostly she was a television watcher. When Norton was home, ensconced before the football games, Marta was a furious knitter of unnecessary sweaters.

In the silent kitchen, a fast gulp of orange juice, and black coffee helped slow down the room to a vague spin, before the walls stopped and became faded wallpaper.

Norton strode in, showered and suited, smelling of after shave, looking pleased with himself and offering his usual good morning joke. "Who's hiding in that robe besides you, some monk?" Thereupon he sat down to his two sunny-side-up eggs, the open sports page beside the plate, his absorbed silence punctuated only by a growl of dismay or satisfaction over scores.

At 7:30, Norton stood at the front door, managing a sidelong glance into the strip of vestibule mirror, pulling up the shoulders, sucking in the paunch. Marta waited patiently for the unnecessary reminder: This being Thursday and bowling night, he'd go right on to the alley, eat something there, save her from cooking.

Raising a hand in a cheerful parting gesture, Norton sailed out into the misty morning, wearing the salesman smile he would use all day, except in traffic, behind the wheel of his red, '56 restored Thunderbird.

With the kitchen back in order, she poured herself a second mug of coffee, put a fat cheese Danish on a small plate and marched to the recliner in front of the TV to begin her free day.

Only once had she gone to the bowling alley to watch. All that hollow, echoing noise made her shudder. The team carried on like overgrown ten-year-olds when Sheena Fast actually made a strike. Sheena was the only female on the office team. The whooping and yipping was for Sheena's jeaned bottom, wiggling with each throw. Marta had walked out to sit in the car and listen to the Classic Hour on the radio, hoping she wasn't running down the battery.

With the plate of Danish and coffee mug in reach, she clicked on the remote control and leaned back with benumbed relief.

A double line of children somewhere in Iowa were jumping up and down behind their school banner chorusing, "Good Morning America!"

In the midst, toward the right, a little old lady in a big brimmed hat, tied with a blowing scarf, gestured wildly at the camera. Marta stared, a catch in her throat. The woman looked for the world like her mother, Ruby, who had worn hats like that. Pushing her way up closer to the camera now, she seemed to be mouthing, "Get up from there, Martie, where's your spunk?"

Hot coffee sloshed in her lap, right through the robe. Marta set the mug down carefully, and leaned in close. The face under the hat might have been Ruby herself as Iowa faded, and the weather man came on.

She muted the sound and took deep breaths, reached for her coffee again. The little woman in the Iowa crowd had surely *looked* like her own dead mother. The big brimmed hat, decorated with a silk scarf the way Ruby always did before she took to her bed upstairs and died up there three years later, which was now four years ago.

She clicked the remote back on. News now. A bunch of pro-life protesters milled around in front of some clinic. One man lay curled on the ground. The camera panned and stopped on a woman in a tailored suit with an old fashioned jabot-type blouse and Harlequin glasses. She looked like Mrs. Euler, a favorite English teacher from high school, thirty-five years ago.

Why, this woman turning to the camera now could be Mrs. Euler's double, complete with that New Yorkish accent, saying right into the camera, "Now I'm for life and choices too—but that means making some choices about what you're going to do about your own life. I've seen too many bright young woman in my time act like sleeping beauties. . . ."

The scene faded. A commercial came on. Under the robe, Marta felt goose bumps. Back there in high school, Mrs. Euler had written that very thing on more than one of her papers. In red ink, she'd scrawled, "You have a good mind, Marta, but you are too passive. You are a sleeping beauty. Wake up."

Doubtful compliment or not, those notes had been saved. Never had she explained to Mrs. Euler it seemed safer to be quiet when your crazy parents made too much noise. A blustery father, an embarrassing mother who was always threatening to run away to Paris or Broadway.

A laxative commercial jumped about on the screen, a woman bouncing around in morning sunshine saying, "Wake up to a new day." The face zoomed in, winking. "And that goes for you."

Click. She sat deeper in the chair, breathing hard, heart pounding. Could vertigo every morning do something to the brain? Spin you eventually into a different orbit? This time, it must have left her out there, looking back, seeing the overstuffed brown couch and chairs as slumped old men with fat eyes closed. The walls weren't spinning. The room and air too dead still.

Had she been getting too little exercise? Polishing the kitchen floor, vacuuming the whole house every other day must not be enough. Saturday mornings they went in the T-Bird to the supermarket but during the week she pushed a basket to a small store, three blocks and back. Or was it what she was eating, all that pot roast and potatoes for Norton. She clicked the television back on.

Didn't you have plans, dreams? Look where you are, some actor was asking a crumpled person behind bars.

Of course she had. Dreams, anyway. Like being an interior designer. And driving around in the English Cotswolds in spring. Studying metaphysics. Marrying a professor who would be both romantic and a fount of knowledge, yet interested in her opinions. Also, she'd always wanted a good woman friend who'd be close as a sister, since she'd been a lonely only child and too quiet in college to fit into any group.

And, yes, she'd dreamed of any number of silly kid things she'd never tried. Like rolling down a grassy slope, over and over, like abandonment to some kind of freedom.

Now the TV screen was showing the President in the Rose Garden, at a mike, looking straight out at her, with a quirk of a smile, intoning, "Now is the time to accomplish this. Move out of this stalemate we've allowed. . . . We can wait no longer. . . ."

The camera backed off to show the crowd circling around. A little woman turned toward the screen, face shaded by a big brimmed hat with a scarf. There was her mother, Ruby, looking straight at her, nodding at what the President was saying.

Marta answered right back: "But I had to take care of you, remember, Mama?"

Click. In the dead silent room, she stood up, dizzy in a different way. The Danish looked repulsive on the dish.

Holding up the long robe, she went down the narrow hall and up the back stairs to the big attic. The past was closed off up there. One side used to be Norton's pool room when his daughter was still living with them, the two of them spending every night up there, fussing and joking and shooting pool. The other side was supposed to be her sewing room where she'd get around some day to making beautiful pillows to sell to shops.

The room had stayed what it had been, Ruby's quarters. At least they had become friends those years when she climbed the stairs with Ruby's trays.

"We women should have more sense," her mother had admitted, propped up in bed, a frail old thing with bright snappy eyes.

"I married a ladies' man who lied through his teeth. You married an insurance salesman dull as dial-tone, who thinks a paycheck is his ticket to meals on time. In this day and age! I might have been too bitchy and drove your daddy off, but if you'd had my sassy streak, you wouldn't be in this fix."

Never, never, had she let Ruby know the marriage had been a two-sided deal, a bargain she had to keep. Marry Norton, put up with his daughter until the girl left. In return, this house had meant a place for her mother to stay and take her own sweet time about dying.

Toward the end, Ruby was still a talker, but out of her head. "You don't have to do all this work. Let's get somebody in here to cook for old Norton. I'll take you to Paris with me. Or we could go see Broadway. Always wanted to do that."

"I know, Mama. What about money?" Mistake, that led to more crazy talk.

"Oh, I have plenty. Somewhere. Back when I was selling Glamour At Home products, I did real good. A rich old fellow paid me extra to paint up his wife regularly."

"Sure he did. You want rice or potato tonight?"

"I pinched it away. Can't remember where I put it. Wasn't going to give it to any bank."

Oh, poor Mama Ruby. She meant well there at the end.

At the top steps, bracing herself for musty air and memories, Marta threw open the door to the gray morning light of her mother's room. The sewing machine, the empty bed, and above it, the shelf piled with boxes and Ruby's hats.

Somewhere up there were her own saved things. She pulled a stool to the window, at the end of the bed, draped the hem of the heavy robe over her arm and climbed up, clutching the shelf to steady herself.

At that moment—chance or subconscious choice?—she looked down and out the window in time to see

Norton's red Thunderbird start out of Sheena Fast's side yard five houses away.

Fascinated, she watched, holding onto the shelf, stool wobbling under her feet. The T-Bird crawled out the back way, turned into the alley, then whipped on out as Norton zoomed down the gray street. With her hard grasp, teetering stool, the shelf dipped. Boxes began sliding off.

Feet caught in the robe, Marta went airborne, landing on the bed in the clutter of cardboard and tin candy boxes and their spilled contents.

She sat up in the mess, listening to her pounding heart.

Well. So that's why Norton had been going out early these mornings, whistling under his breath. The knowledge seemed curious and interesting, for reasons not yet assimilated.

She sat there, picking up first one, then another scrap from the past—a big brimmed Ruby hat, a packet of letters from foreign pen pals, small journals begun and never finished, a poem clipped to a contest entry, never sent. A form for course information at the local university, not mailed.

From the open high school album, her picture looked up—a pretty girl with big eyes and uncertain smile, and caption: "Marta plans to be an interior designer and develop English connections." Stuck in place same page, a newspaper clipping from the school paper about the school play where she had a walk-on part, only it never happened. The clip said: "Great Expectations Show Postponed."

Sheena Fast! Well, that wasn't a surprise. Sheena, forty, divorced, with a rambunctious eight-year-old boy who careened up and down the street on his bike. Sheena, stridently blonde, with no likely boyfriend and stuck in a dead-end job, and having to bowl for something to do with her Thursday and Saturday nights. Norton probably looked the most likely, barrel-chested, grinning, showing up with a wife only once.

Ruby's Greta Garbo hat seemed to have a scarf sewed inside the crown like a heavy sachet. Ruby's Gardenia perfume lifted in the still air as Marta pulled the thing loose, and opened it. Money. Green bills, pinched into little packets. Saved over how long back there hustling around in her beat-up Volkswagen selling cosmetics. There must have been a daft old man paying her to fix up his wife. Fifties here, hundreds, rolled tight in rubber bands.

Ruby's Paris money. Oh, her poor, dear, wild dreamer of a mother. There was enough here to run away somewhere, but where? Paris wouldn't do her a bit of good. Something had to be done about Norton and Sheena. She stuffed the whole bunch of bills into the now empty, tin candy box. Sat it on the top of the sewing machine. Went out, shut the door, shivering.

Holding up the heavy robe, she limped downstairs. Took the robe off, stuffed it in the garbage, stood in her nightgown like a stranger looking at the kitchen. What a pale, drab place. Why hadn't she done something colorful in here? One little pot of African violets sat on the windowsill, dying in the wrong light.

The living room now. Chairs and couch still looking like squat old men. Norton had grown up with this stuff here in his mother's house. Came back to it after a divorce with an eleven-year-old daughter. Housekeepers had come and gone, she knew because he'd shown up at the employment agency, where Marta had her first dumb job. He'd sat across from her desk with his big chest and salesman smile, looking for help. Had come back again, wanting to take her for a ride in one of his classic cars.

Not long after, walking into this house as a bride, hadn't she suggested making some changes? "Why spend money to replace good stuff?" Norton had said. The last housekeeper had made him buy a new washer, dryer and stove.

The blank-faced television waited like a challenge. Marta grabbed the remote and clicked it on. Some soap opera beauty was shrugging in distaste. "You've been living like this? What happened to your love of color?"

The other actress looked remorseful. "It seemed safe. Roger said. . . ."

"And you, fool, believed him? Don't you know how long this has been going on with that girl? You've got to get rid of him."

Marta heard her own protest: *Don't you tell me to go shoot him, just because you can do it on TV.*

The TV wife sobbed: "But how?" The friend moved in for a close-up: "First, you have to imagine him gone."

She unplugged the set. In the bedroom, she made the beds with meticulous care, imagining Norton gone. Dressed as if she had someplace to go, still imagining Norton gone. Not dead, but gone, like a door shut behind him. And the door open for her. To go where? The thought was more dizzying than morning vertigo.

The doorbell rang. A young rosy-cheeked policeman stood there with nervous hands and apologetic frown. Outside, a Pinellas County Sheriff's cruiser waited.

"Mrs. Norton Treadwell? Sorry Ma'am, don't get upset now, because he's all right, but your husband had a little accident this morning. He's been taken to the emergency at Bayfront, but they'll be keeping him. He's probably okay because going on the stretcher he was shouting about suing the kids who ran into him. He might have a couple of broken legs. I told him we would let you know, take you down if you like. Are you going to be all right? Would you like to go now?"

Yes, she'd go. Took her raincoat and purse and followed him to the cruiser. Oh, poor Norton. She'd almost killed him by wishing him gone.

She found him in his hospital bed, red-faced and cussing, both legs encased and tied up to some contraption. Sat there listening and nodding to his wounded dignity and voluble rage over the totaled T-Bird. He'd had the top down. The impact sent him flying into the street. All because he had passed a slow-moving old geezer in an '83 Buick and didn't get back into the lane before those blasted kids came at him.

"You'd better leave," Norton groaned. "I'm about to puke."

Marta walked out with his list of requirements, some long tee-shirts rather than the godawful gown, his shaver, nose spray and toothbrush. In the hall, the doctor showed up, heavy brows knitted, announcing her husband might be in for a lengthy stay. Landing on the pavement had done more to Norton than break both legs. He'd be in a back cast for some time. Might be moved over to the Veterans' Administration Hospital since it could mean as long as three months.

If the young policeman remembered to come back for her, Marta didn't wait to find out. She needed to get outside, to walk, and deal with a curious mix of guilt. Not only had she almost killed Norton, she was feeling strangely happy he was tied up. A sense of buoyancy came with the thought of possibly three months of freedom. To do what?

My calm story teller leaned back to say, "This was Marta on that March day. Would you care to hear what happened in the three months that followed?"

I did. "Though she sounds too benumbed to make choices. Are you going to tell me there's a guardian angel who arranges fate for hapless females?"

"Or do moments come when fate and choice have to recognize each other? Shall I go on?"

I said, "Oh yes." Outside the rain still lashed at the street. . . .

From the hospital, Marta struck out, walking the six miles back to the house. The rain had stopped, the day fresh and blustery. At first she tracked along at a fast clip, guilt and pleasure hovering at her back. Sheena Fast popped up in her mind but faded as quickly. At the moment Sheena didn't seem pertinent.

Avoiding the highway, she headed home, winding her way through the old downtown neighborhood she knew mostly from a car window. An old Carnegie library set back on a lawn. Here was something to do with this freedom; go in, and read about the Cotswolds. She didn't get farther than the entrance. Embarrassment sent her right back out.

Continuing on—the morning too special to stay miserable—she walked down old sidewalks, under ragged palms, feeling like a mystery woman, an amnesia victim in a TV movie, lost but not caring, plastic rain coat flapping open, her eyes the camera focusing on these new sights. As a passenger in the T-Bird, gazing out in a private haze, she'd never noticed all of this. Once family homes with porches now cut into apartments. Small mom and pop stores turned into open door laundry places or vegetable stands. Dogs came out yipping and followed awhile. She patted cats who came close, and spotted others watching.

Here and there, a stop to rest turned out to be a visit with strangers who talked back like friends, the whole strange day happening like pieces of a new puzzle.

It was late afternoon, the air turning cold when she dragged herself into the tomb of the silent house. A weary silence, and in the quiet, the goose-pimply sense that her mother was upstairs, Ruby-like, waiting to hear what happened.

The blank-faced television waited, a hated friend. Just to check, she clicked the thing on, willing for noisy commercials to supply giddy voices.

A talk show blared out. Some woman expert was telling a whimpering guest, "You say what's happened to you seems unfair fate, or senseless puzzle. No—everything that happens does so for a reason. Try seeing the pattern, the message. . . ."

She jerked the cord out of the base socket. Shivering, she went into the silent kitchen. Looked into the refrigerator at left over chicken dumplings. No. Walked out with a carrot.

In the silent bathroom, as the tub filled, she stood naked, looking at this dislocated self in the same old body. Eating the carrot, she sank into the hot depths, a pleasure seldom afforded herself. It was comfort now, for re-thinking the whole day.

Until she heard her crazy mama, Ruby-like, asking, *Well—what happened?*

Marta didn't move, but sank deeper in the hot water. If she sat up, looked back beyond the rim of the tub, she would surely see Ruby, wrapped in her Chinese dressing gown, eyes big in her scrawny expectant face, waiting to hear everything. She didn't have to look.

Go on, daughter, speak up, what all happened after you found out about Norton?

Your kind of day, Mama. Crazy.

So tell me. . . .

And Marta reported, for her own and Ruby's benefit.

First, that stop at the little Carnegie Library. Five silk-suited, fussy hair-doed women sat behind a table, selling tickets to their benefit tea, raising funds to purchase the old Tyndale house for their garden club headquarters.

Now there's something different you could have done, daughter, with old Norton tied up the way he is, getting his supper on a hospital tray.

Yes, she'd stood there considering that very ridiculous possibility. Except the women kept talking in each other's faces, carefully ignoring any lumpy woman in a plastic raincoat with tied-back stringy hair. Yes, she'd left.

Snooty old biddies, hope they scratched up their old Cadillacs on the way out. What happened next?

Gloria, the Italian woman at the fruit stand, was cheerful enough to make up for the garden clubbers. Gloria washed the grapes and a pear before putting them in the bag.

Five blocks on, looked for a place to rest and eat her grapes. No sidewalk bench in sight. Poked her head in the open door of a cubby hole real estate office. A wiry little fellow sitting inside behind his desk, elbows propped, face in his hands, waved her in. Solly Berger shared her grapes, brought out his own cheese and crackers, and cups of coffee. She sat there resting and listening to his whole life story and about his daughter, the lawyer, whose picture smiled out of a frame on his desk. Listening to Solly was as good as reading a book of somebody's life. Helped her forget her own.

Some of us with gumption need to talk. You haven't talked enough, Marty. Go on....

Six blocks farther down, there was a bus stop bench, shady with trees growing behind a fancy iron gate. Soon as she sat down gratefully, here came a perky little woman, silver hair tucked under her gold plastic rain hat. Parked herself on the bench.

Another talker, I bet.

Mehitable was her name. Hetty to her friends, only too many had died off who knew her as Hetty, she'd explained. Now people think she's a stubborn old woman because she still has a mind of her own. Has a son up north, worried about her living down here by herself and refusing to give up the house.

And you said. . .?

Hetty, you're a lot like my mother, Ruby. You two would have been great friends.

True, true. And she. . .?

Said she'd settle for being friends with the daughter. So I told her about the garden club women, but not about Norton. Already I was doing a good job wishing Norton away.

Wishing is one thing. Doing is another, Marty. Go on. . .

Hetty knew all about the garden club women who wanted to buy the Tyndale house. She turned around, nodding to the three-story yellow brick house, built when this neighborhood was in its prime, now almost hidden behind an iron gate. Hetty said the garden clubbers were always bugging her son Reggie to sell it, turn it over at a gift price, just to have the Tyndale name on a plaque in front. Bugging her too, asking her to their social doings.

Sounds like you were sitting with mama Tyndale.

Yes, resting and listening to Hetty tell about that sweet old place where she'd raised two boys, lost one and a husband. Son Reggie couldn't sell it and make her move into some new condominium because her name was still on the deed, along with his.

And you said. . . ?

I told her how as a child I'd dreamed of living in a place like that, as if it were my own small castle on a green slope I could roll down. . .

And Hetty said. . .?

She thought I sounded like a girl with imagination and spunk. Said she still had her own spunk, only Reggie wouldn't trust her to use it, living alone the way she does. Comes in and out the back way. Sits out there to watch people.

That woman is lonely. So go on . . .

Marta added more hot water, carefully not looking back at Ruby, waiting to hear more. Especially about the last stop. The sign had said Old and New Dreams.

Second-hand-Rose place. Oh, they're the best. So tell me. . . .

Six more blocks down an old store, windows filled with a conglomeration—a sequined gown, books, colored glass vases, an old fox fur neck piece. Yes, and a pile of hats.

Inside, a short round woman in a purple muu-muu, a big straw hat with flowers on her rust red head, stood behind her counter, gluing odd pieces of jewelry into bizarre brooches. That was Rhonda—". . .named myself after Rhonda Fleming."

My kind of person. Tell me about Rhonda.

Had this shop crammed with stuff. Costumey clothes, piles of hats, shoes, an alcove of books with one recliner chair, about as large as a closet.

My kind of place. Hope you stayed to look around. . .

Found the bathroom in the back that used to be a beauty shop. Yes, looked around. At fashion finery bunched up on the racks. Rhonda explained they come in from rich women who need to empty their closets so they can keep shopping for the new.

And the hats. Try one on for your Mama?

One with brown ostrich feathers from some belle of the ball fifty years ago. It didn't go with the plastic raincoat. Rhonda shook her head, agreeing. Said: "Honey, you're looking for something, but you've got to find it before you're ready to be sassy."

Told her I did have problems on my mind.

Go on, Marty. A woman like that has ideas.

Rhonda said I'd find all the answers I'm looking for in the alcove. Meaning sitting in there with those old books.

Bet she told you why you needed to sit in there...

Told me to sit in the chair, lean back, feet up, and think of the question that needs an answer. Then pick up a book, any one your hand lands on and scan a couple of pages. If nothing leaps out at you, put it back and take down another. Do it with an open mind and your answer will pop right up—maybe like silver italics getting your attention. If, that is, you're not impatient. If you're open, ready for answers.

Daughter, I hope you didn't say Rhonda was talking through her hats and walk out of there....

Told her I'd come back and try her alcove some other day. She wagged her hatted head, shrugged, and said people always say they'll get around to solving a problem then they keep right on following their noses.

I like that woman. And you...?

So I sat in her alcove. Put my tired feet up. Looked around at the books, the kind with old covers. Had so many questions in my mind that day they were bumping into to each other.

So you tried her alcove ...

The recliner felt good. Maybe I dozed thinking again how the whole day was like pieces of a puzzle and what did that have to do with Norton and Sheena Fast? Finally pulled out a musty book. Put it back. Opened another book. Ralph Waldo Emerson.

A line did leap up: "All persons are puzzles until at last we find in some word or act the key . . . straightway all their words and actions lie in light before us."

Closed that book, sat there, then pulled out another, opened it at random. Bertrand Russell: "The mind is a strange machine which can combine the materials offered in most astonishing ways."

Tried another very old volume. Someone called the Earl of Rochester was saying: "Since 'tis Nature's lair to change . . . Constancy alone is strange."

Marty, you hear me daughter? Didn't I tell you years back—being stuck doesn't mean you have to stay stuck?

Questions got clearer anyway. So I cracked open another book asking: . . . How to get rid of Norton without guilt? Read it quick and closed it fast.

The line that popped up: "Don't solve a problem on the level of the problem." Einstein.

On this rainy evening inside the Boston bookstore, my hostess paused in her storytelling. We were quiet for a moment, listening to rain.

"That was Marta Treadwell on her fateful March day. The next morning she didn't have vertigo. Knew she wouldn't have it for three months. But she didn't see a way out of her stuck situation."

"Of habit called duty."

"Yes. Do you think she made it?"

I looked at this woman waiting there, lamplight glowing on the smooth sweep of champagne hair.

"You're smiling so I think she did. But in three months?"

"Perhaps there comes a time when fate forces one—or offers one—the prod and inspiration to make choices. Like this." And she finished her story.

Fate was not having a car. Choice had Marta walking every day, to get out of the house, even when Norton was moved to the VA further away and he growled, she need not try to take a bus there, except to bring his mail.

On those fine spring days, she made her regular stops. At Gloria's for fruit, tracking on to visit Solly, hear his stories. . . . On down the narrow shaded streets to sit on the bench with Hetty . . . before stopping in at Rhonda's where she bought a new dress, size 14, not 16. Then back to the drab silent cocoon of a house, to soak in the hot water, eating pecans and carrots.

Four weeks later, getting off the bus at the VA Hospital with Norton's mail, she saw Sheena Fast coming out of his room. In Rhonda's alcove, she'd read: *Make use of the problem, don't bury it.*

That evening, she knocked on Sheena's front door. Seeing her there, the girl stood bug-eyed and suspicious, listening to the message. Which was: Norton needed all his bowling pals to visit, he loved chocolate cake if anyone cared to bring some along, and when Sheena went, she might tell Norton his mail was being forwarded there, because Marta was taking off to stay with an old cousin. The last a lie, but the harmless useful variety.

Sheena blinked and nodded at this unsuspected invitation to move in on Norton. Marta surprised herself by adding: "He's a good man. Doesn't want to miss any of his bills." Sheena smiled weakly and closed the door.

By April, Marta moved into Tyndale place in one of the big unused bedrooms. Friend Hetty was lonely in that big house, living in only one part of it, eating at the diner every night. Thinking of Ruby's Paris money, Marta had offered to buy an interest in Tyndale house, so she could vote with Hetty against selling it.

Hetty thought that a sweet thing but said, no, Marta could pay rent if she liked.

By late April, still doing her walking, and keeping Hetty company in the afternoons, and sleeping nights in a four-poster bed in the Tyndale house, Marta knew she couldn't go back in that place with Norton. Solly's daughter, the lawyer, drew up the no-fault divorce papers to be delivered to the hospital.

Marta added a nice letter telling Norton he was a good man but deserved someone who enjoyed sports and bowling; and she would be fine since she'd found some money Ruby left in a hat. There was no reason to tell him how much.

53

Solly's daughter helped Marta change her name from Treadwell back to her maiden name.

By April 15, unsure how her wishes were developing, Marta called the nurse's desk on Norton's floor to inquire about his progress. She was told he was progressing, though still in the cast. "His wife visits every day. She's in there now. Want to talk to her?"

Marta said no thanks and hung up with great relief. She was getting rid of both Norton and Sheena. But what if Sheena went looking through the house? She'd want to run from that tomb. So she had Solly Berger look it over and write up a contract to send to Norton. "Just in case he is interested in selling," she explained. "But mail it right after he sends back the divorces papers signed."

First of May, the garden club ladies were on the phone to Hetty wanting to give a luncheon in her honor. "Trying to butter me up," Hetty told Marta. "I'll go if you go with me, as my secretary and friend."

At Old Dreams and New, Rhonda helped her pick out a suit with a Saks label inside. Size 12 this time. Rhonda danced a little hip-swinging jig. "Must have saved this for you. You're already past sassy hats, my friend. You're already at serene elegance. Goes with the hair, too."

The second treatment in the bathroom behind the alcove had left it a nice Champagne Gold.

The tea was rather fun, the women buzzing around Hetty Tyndale and respectfully hovering around her private secretary Marta, who was finding serene elegance came easy if you claimed it. She told them exactly what the Tyndale house was worth, quoting Solly.

Reggie Tyndale showed up a week later, a blond fellow with intense blue eyes and a worried look. He'd just gone through his most recent divorce. He wanted to know: "Mother, who is this woman living here?"

"She's my friend, my secretary when I need one, and she's going to be my traveling companion," Hetty told him. "We're going to England so she can walk around the Cotswolds and I can sit in front of a pub and watch people. You'll meet her. She's out walking. Back in time for dinner. We always go to the diner."

Reggie took them both out to a downtown dinner place. Before he left, Reggie announced with relief or concession, "I'll give up worrying about you, Mother, now that you have a sensible friend in the house. Nice woman, but quiet. Maybe has to be, listening to you. All right, we keep the house until you're ready to sell."

Marta's confident look was still new as the champagne hair but it settled in, as a natural thing, once the signed divorce papers came back to Solly's office.

Behind the wheel of Hetty's old Cadillac weeks later, Marta drove along the familiar street. Solly's For Sale sign was still stuck in front, with a new sold sign attached. A second hand furniture truck sat out front. Hopefully, Sheena hadn't had a chance to look inside.

By passing later, she spied a stiff-legged Norton in front of Sheena's place, making Sheena's boy push the lawnmower.

My story-telling hostess leaned back in her chair, with a rueful smile. "You're a good listener."

"So we get back to: fate forces choice and choice becomes fate." We were quiet for minutes like comfortable friends who understand one another.

I still had questions.

"When did all this happen?"

"Three years ago."

I picked up the card that said Pamela Wessner.

She smiled. "My given name—Martha Pamela. I left poor Marta behind."

"That was in Florida, wasn't it? So what brought you to Boston?"

"Once we'd made a second trip, to Spain, I could tell Hetty was finally ready to sell the old place. The Junior League wanted it for a city museum. They paid a fair price. I was ready to start my business. Yes, with Ruby's Paris money. Reggie was up here. It seemed a good place to open my shop."

I looked at the books behind her head. "So now you have walls of 'marvelous secrets.' Inspired by Rhonda's alcove."

"Actually, they aren't secrets. Wisdom about our human condition is not new. It's always been there, not only in sacred texts but from many minds though the ages who have put down their thoughts. The only secret is, one has to re-discover it, and be open to what it applies."

"You didn't stay stuck."

"No."

The front door jiggled. In came a raincoated blond fellow with intense blue eyes. He looked at home here. "Storm's slowing but it's still coming down. Oh, hello. Mother's in the car, Pam. She still expects to go out for dinner, rain or not."

I got up to go, asking about a phone to call for a cab. My hostess said, "Oh, Reggie can drop you off at the hotel."

I glanced out at a sleek town car. Before he came back in to bring umbrellas, I had to ask. "I supposed Norton and Sheena married?"

She grimaced. "Who? Here's Reggie. You go first and meet Hetty. I'll be turning off the lights."

Marian Coe

Concessions

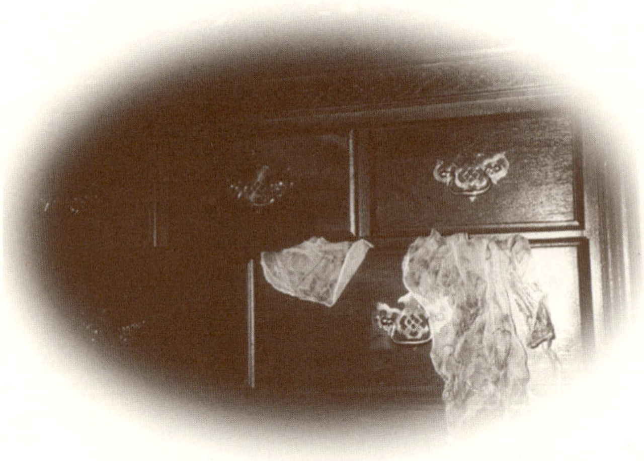

Concessions

Just look at her, Emma fumes under her breath, as she bustles in and out of the living room where Sarah sits.

Look at her sitting there like Miss Important, expecting me to bring her a scarf from the top bureau drawer. As if it mattered, how dressed up she is, for a doctor's visit, at that. That's the way it is with people who think they're so smart. They expect to have everything their way, and leave worrying about practical things up to people like me. Appreciated or not, I do worry about Sarah. Did all those years she had her fancy job in New York, even before she came down here to live with me.

I invited her, that's true. I'm not one to turn my back on a sister. The fact her eyes started going bad right after she moved into my front room, well, that's just another burden the Lord has put on me and, before it's over, Sarah will have earned me more stars in my crown.

Why, I wouldn't have known about this new trouble if I hadn't been watching, if I hadn't noticed how Sarah would get this far-away look and funny little smile while I was talking. I had to *make* her tell me.

She was *having visions* of all things. My sister Sarah, right here in my house, is *seeing* things in her head and if Jimmy will ever show up, we're taking her to a doctor. This very afternoon. Though it means I'm giving up Oprah and my stories. I'm not one to shirk my Christian duty.

"Did you find my scarf?" Sarah asks with smiling forbearance, sitting here dressed and ready, except for the scarf, clicking her nails on the arm of the chair when Emma doesn't answer.

Ah, well, I shall wait. I did not ask for this excursion, did not wish to see any doctor. I regret ever admitting to my sister about the visions. I rather enjoy them. In Emma's officious way, she insisted on this appointment with a neurologist and has delegated my poor nephew to take us there. Jimmy is late of course, a fact Emma tries to ignore by bustling about, mumbling and complaining. I take pride in the fact I have learned long ago to screen out annoyances. Here it is a necessity.

One learns to make concessions.

The fact of my failing eyesight upsets Emma more than it does me. At least now the reality of my situation here has a nicely dimmed quality. This room, for example. When I came, the mirror over the stuffed couch made me shudder. It's a blatant thing, framed in plastic gold, repeating the bad taste of the room.

The garish glitter is quite subdued for me now, for which I can only be thankful. I don't need it to know the Chanel suit I'm wearing still looks good, though it does needs a bit of softness at the neck.

Oh yes, I use the eye drops, but the grayness increases. The scenes, which I find more interesting, appear at the bottom of my vision, when they happen. The images are really quite clear. Strange ones, but quite intriguing.

You don't need any scarf, Emma says, huffing back into the room, Dacron dress rustling, the heat of her body fired by impatience, probably over Jimmy's lateness. She will not complain about him in front of me. The boy is her sole proof of accomplishment in life. Mine, she would say, was merely a career. Ended of course.

"I told you just where it was. In the top bureau drawer," I say, keeping my voice precise but softly modulated. I have always taken pride in my voice. My sister's high, petulant tone must come from home-bound years of maternal duty. It carries the squeak of unrecognized protest.

"You're not going to be on TV for heaven's sakes, you're going to the doctor."

"Right, Emma." I let it sound amused. "I'm no longer *on* TV now, just sitting in front of it like everyone else."

Thirty-five years ago I sent her a picture of myself, smiling out of *Life* pages. I wore a Chanel suit, little scarf at the throat, doing some interview show. A mistake, I'm sure, but how did I know at the time?

We women were a rare breed in the national media then. That picture must have arrived at an inopportune time. Poor Emma probably opened it with a crying baby in her lap and a husband complaining supper wasn't ready. I shouldn't have written later, when he left, "good riddance, Emma." I do not point out such things now. Besides, women like Emma are too fortified with matriarchal righteousness to hear someone else's opinion if it differs from her own.

Jimmy's car whips up to the front. A door slams. I can always judge my nephew's mood. He walks in breathing hard, impatient to get the chore over, saying, "Hi, Mama. Hi, Aunt Sarah. You two ready? Let's get moving."

Jimmy prances around while Emma gets her purse. I am sure he is wondering if I'm going to do something strange. The boy is in electronics and does well, but in a discussion of politics or personalities where subtleties are involved, he is as lost as his mother. "Emma is forcing this on both of us," I say sweetly toward his hazy shape.

She hears that. "As long as you're in my care. . ." Emma begins in that noble voice with the slight quiver.

I realize she is afraid I could be losing my mind. And Emma is a woman who has to have every chair and dish in place, and every fact obvious, her household in her control.

Her fears have a certain contagion. I have always been a practical person, organized, impatient with day dreams. I admit these visions are a matter of unsettling curiosity. So I have consented to this afternoon exercise.

In the car, Jimmy asks again, "You all right back there, Aunt Sarah? Mother, pull that seat belt out, remember, before you try to hook it. Aunt Sarah?"

"I'm here, Jimmy. I'm not running away."

We crunch out the driveway and into the hum of traffic. I lean back in my gray fog. How much should I tell the doctor? I try to see my shoes in the depths of the back seat. Low level sight I still have. So in Emma's house, I see too much of the waxed floors.

Until the visions started. That's where I see them, eyes down. At this moment, I lean against the window and see gray asphalt moving past. I actually wish it would happen again, one more time, before the doctor medicates me back to sanity.

Jimmy is asking, "Does it happen very often—this seeing things, Aunt Sarah?"

"Let's don't talk about it," Emma snaps.

"I just wondered," Jimmy says.

"Well, don't."

I turn off their talk to an inaudible hum and lean back, looking again at vague passing asphalt. Without warning, it starts. The low band of vision clears more and shows me a cobblestone street and now sandaled feet moving along. I look for the two children sitting on stone steps of some kind of a temple. Two grubby girls, always there, as if they wait for me, as the togas pass by. I want to see more, see the rest of the picture, what's above them, I believe, is a temple door.

The visions fade as we pull up an incline and Jimmy's voice barks out orders. "We're parking here on ramp A-7 left of the elevator so everybody remember that."

From the elevator we walk down a long hall that smells of new carpeting. What a cool, sterile place this building, compared to the ones I remember, newsrooms that crackled with tension like a pulse beat with the heat of lights and trappings of cameras. The momentum drove you, kept you so high, you didn't mind coming home drained, alone, to the hush of an apartment.

Those same years Emma's Christmas cards included her sisterly warnings. "No life for a woman." Or peppery condolences on a second divorce. "When will you learn! You can't be so stubborn and opinionated and keep a husband." She had to add, of course, that in her own case it couldn't be helped, "Not after that sugary little secretary turned his head. But you, Miss Big Time, you will be sorry. Someday you'll need a real home."

Yes, I have done her the favor. She has the pleasure of thinking she has been proven right. Emma needs someone to boss and fuss over. In return, the room is nice, the bed is good, windows open to fragrant foliage. Her cat has adopted me. Sister means well and cooks better. I have not deserted my principles of independence. I have yielded to accommodation. Problems come with benefits. Soon after the glaucoma began, so did the visions.

The waiting room smells of tweed fabric and false chilled air. We wait. "I'm going in alone," I tell the person who comes out to call my name.

Emma fusses, but the young woman says brightly, "You're family? Just wait out here and the doctor will talk to you after he sees our patient here." Her hand is warm on my arm.

Inside another chilled room, from a deep chair, I show her how poised I am in spite of being led about though this dimness. I thank her with my dignity intact. "My sister is a bossy woman, over zealous in her caretaker role." I see the hazy face is smiling as she leans forward to take down my history. She is the doctor's assistant, not a clerk, so I am quite willing to talk freely to the rustling pad.

"My complaint? Actually, I am not here with a complaint, but rather curiosity. I am mystified and even entertained by these hallucinations. They seem quite real. My sister fears I'm losing my mind, which I have no intention of doing. But since I am living in her house—here I am. I suppose you have drugs that can take away the visions."

"Tell me about them, what do you see?" The voice has the quality of warm caring, without judgment.

So I tell her about the cobblestone street, the passing feet in sandals. Yes, I've traveled, I say, but this is not a memory of Rome or Greece with little Fiats whipping by. I see cracks in the cobblestones and the dirty steps where the grubby children sit. People hurry by in togas, not costumes. There is a momentum. It is a place.

The doctor walks in, with his false greeting, sounding hurried. He murmurs and turns the pages of the assistant's notes and asks questions. I give him a shortened version. The young woman remains quiet but her presence is a comfort. The doctor's smooth tenor sounds brusque now, talking about erratic mental reaction due to emotional stress, due to changes in one's life.

"Your loss of vision from glaucoma is a trauma you apparently have yet to fully accept." He scratches something on his pad. A prescription for some kind of tranquilizer I'm to take at night. Something that should calm the nervous system, aid sleep, he says, "while you are adjusting to your situation."

Emma is called in. I don't try to focus her pursed mouth, don't try to hear her chatter of satisfaction as she takes charge of the moment and collects the prescription.

With Jimmy and Emma waiting at the front desk to finish, the young woman walks me toward the elevator, arms linked as if she were a daughter. It gives me a shiver of loneliness, a sense of something lost, but disciplined as I am, I put that aside and ask casually, "Will the medication stop my errant pictures?" And she says, "Yes, it calms the nervous system. Your pictures can go away, if you wish."

In the car again, sounding pleased with herself, my sister orders Jimmy to stop at the drug store before going home. "Sarah has to start taking those things before she goes to bed. And hurry, I've missed Oprah but I'm not going to miss bingo tonight."

In the back seat, I smile at Emma's foolish pleasure. Smile because I must admit, Emma's bingo nights are a pleasure for me too. The house is quiet.

Tonight, after Emma leaves, I make my way carefully down the dim hall into the bathroom with the bottle of pills that should take away the pictures. The light has become a harsh haze but it is enough. The prescription bottle holds white pellets. I empty them into the john and flush them away, open the medicine cabinet and get out the bottle in the corner, my muscle relaxer tablets, which I remember are also little white things. I refill the prescription bottle with these and go back to bed.

Some of the most interesting visions come at night when I can see down the cobblestone street beyond the two urchins. I do believe they wait for me. Not adorable children, but contrary little girls who appear to fuss and challenge one another, yet cling to one another as well. They seem familiar, sitting on those stone steps, in wherever time or place I'm seeing.

I want to see them more clearly. This is not the kind of satisfaction or amusement I've known in my life . . . but yes, in the dark, in a silent house, I shall lie in bed and wait with private anticipation.

Homecoming

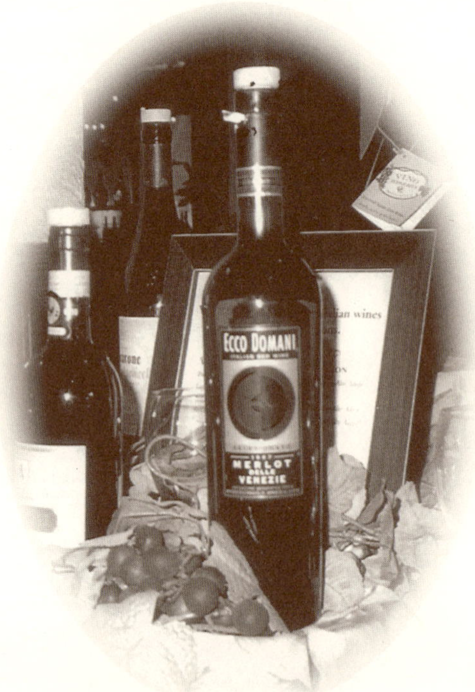
ECCO DOMANI
MERLOT
DELLE
VENEZIE

Homecoming

For Peg Singleton, four years retired now, living alone with her cat, Bailey, the coming week in her daughter's home waits like a wrapped gift, contents unknown, long overdue, and about to be opened.

Tonight's flight to Atlanta leaves at 10:30. At 5:00 she's ready, the cat delivered to a neighbor down the block, the suitcase repacked for the third time. In front of the hall mirror, she scrutinizes herself in the designer suit Carla sent two Christmases ago. Will she remember?

At 5:30, in the living room, she tries to read *Newsweek* but no way, the pulse beat of impatience is too loud against the silence. If this were an ordinary Friday night she'd be going to Luigi's. Well, why not go on there rather than wait here? The airport limo could pick her up at the restaurant.

At 6:00 the cab pulls up under the red neon glow of Luigi's Italian Villa. Plunging into the restaurant's familiar hum and intercom aria, already Peg feels better. She pushes the bag under the coat rack, waits for the rotund man behind the cash register to finish expounding the excellence of his restaurant to a couple of departing customers.

"Not only the best sauce, my friends," Luigi is saying, "but the most loyal customers. Roanoke city council, county commission. Tonight, see that table in the back? That's our own Press Club. Here's one of them now—this little lady here."

The two men regard Peg with stretched, polite smiles. "He means we're a bunch of former by-lines," she says quickly. "Old cronies from the newsroom showing up every Friday for his pasta." She tells Luigi an airport limo will be out front looking for her at 8:30.

The long room is a darkened maze of busy tables. Peg maneuvers through the waves of garlic and Parmesan, trying to judge how many have shown up for the round table in the back. Only three so far. By God, they do look like a bunch of old cronies. Bitchy Nina, heavy shoulders hunched, holding forth, probably about this morning's editorial on the school board. And Tucker, ever the film critic, retired or not, looking more and more like a fragile, silver-haired Errol Flynn. And Johnny, fat fingers tapping some article he's brought.

No Binki, yet. He must still be at Mayo's for the follow-up on his chemo. Sweet old Binki, determined to finish his book about friend Jimmy Carter.

They glance up at her approach, greet her with questions. Isn't this her night to take off for Atlanta? Isn't she due to play grand dame grandma at the debutante ball?

"On my way," Peg says, settling in. "I might as well kill time here over lasagna."

"Deb balls are an anachronism," Nina says in her cigarette-roughened voice. "Some new daddies must have bucks to burn. You males wouldn't remember, but back in the old days of 'women's pages'—Gawd, we had to treat debutante season like the Second Coming. Guess who groaned the loudest having to cover that fluff? Grandma of the deb here."

"You've told them," Peg says, accepting a bread stick and claiming a wine glass. She hasn't seen Tracy in four years, but the deb thing tomorrow night is beside the point. It's the chance to look in on her daughter's life, the opportunity—so long needed—for them to sit down and talk to one another, really talk, eye to eye.

Johnny's pudgy fingers tap her arm. "Bring me an Atlanta paper. And have a fine visit with the daughter."

"About time," Nina says. "Carla never comes *here*. Don't scowl, Peg. I know you don't say anything, but—"

"They have a busy life," Peg says.

She's shown them clippings and snapshots. They know how handsome the family looks on an Aspen ski slope: a smiling Carla, a darkly handsome Jeff, and granddaughter Tracy, taller each year.

"I joined them in Las Vegas a couple of years ago, remember?" Peg says. Then, to the young man at her shoulder with his pad, "Tony, I'll have the usual. And watch for a limo in front for me?"

"Sure, we remember Vegas, don't we?" Nina says. "Two, three days in that circus, as mother-in-law at a bar convention. You hated it."

"The place, yes." She came back to deliver a wry account of lights, crowds, and drunken comedians. The disappointment she'd kept to herself. That frantic scene was an unlikely place for a family reunion, a quiet moment for anything like a personal talk. Back home, she'd phoned Carla and thanked her like a guest.

Nina shrugs her heavy shoulders. "You may be lucky you have to travel to see them. My son Jake piles in on me every time there's a game in town. Trouble is, he brings the daughter-in-law from hell and their kids who don't read. Galling to see that. My offspring has produced MTV and computer freaks."

"How's Binki?" Peg asks.

"Coming back Monday," Johnny says. "Called me yesterday, said he's heading right here. I'm coming in Monday so he won't be alone. Says he'll know then if he's going to live or die and regardless, plans to order the spaghetti with sausage. That's our Binki, hanging in there."

"Don't we all?" Nina says. "Tucker, you'd better pour that wine."

On the flight to Atlanta, among sleeping strangers, Peg feels suspended in limbo, looking out into blackness until the reflection in the window demands her focus. So who is this person now, four years retired? This small neat woman with the short crisp hair. The pleasant expression—is it molded by habit, from thirty years of presenting a public face? This look of unruffled confidence, impervious to hurt? A useful facade, from the time she was a fledgling reporter, hiding insecurities, with a child to support, husband dead.

And the years after? Always, the impervious face was a front for blustering men or the condescending ones or the social strivers, before she went back alone to a late newsroom to write the essence of that meeting, that happening. Could protective habits become the persona?

Those years left plaques on the hall wall and half finished stories and deadlines in her dreams. But she wakes up at three a.m., looking up at a shadowed ceiling asking herself: what do I have to show for those same years of being a parent? Now and then, yes, a pleasant phone call from Carla. But friendly isn't personal.

The plane makes a rough landing. Anticipation tightening her chest, Peg files out with the others into the fluorescent glare and air-conditioned chill of the late hour terminal. Stands there, blinking, watching strangers converge on one another, becoming family clusters. She waits, scanning for a familiar face. A daughter's. Maybe even a granddaughter will show up.

A young man is striding toward her, flashing a smile. Jeff. This hyper forty-five-year-old head of his firm. A man who might be hell to work for, or be grilled by. And married to? She doesn't know that much about their marriage.

Peg moves to meet him, grateful for the brisk hug and rapid greeting. "Carla said she'd try to stay awake until I had you delivered," Jeff says on the down escalators toward the luggage pick-up. "Don't count on it. Tomorrow's a helluva busy day."

In the Mercedes, a silver convertible, they wheel out of the terminal into heavy midnight traffic, Jeff playing jovial host.

"So, Peggy, what does my mother-in-law do with herself these days? Know any loaded silver-haired dudes back there?"

"Quite a few, but not loaded." What to tell her son-in-law that he'd care to hear?—about volunteering at the library, about teaching How to Write Your Life at a senior center? Not likely. Assure him she makes herself swim laps in the condo pool three times a week? No way.

She does have good stories to tell, worth the attention of this assured young man. She has insider stories Johnny shared about his years on the *Wall Street Journal* and Binki tells from his Capitol Hill days during Watergate. Even from that newsroom, she and Nina and Tucker and the rest had covered a changing society through the seventies and eighties. Does it ever occur to the young, taking over the world, that those ahead of them might just have a seasoned insight into the present?

"I live with Bailey," Peg tells Jeff's intent profile. "He's an old tom. Bailey, as in Irish Creme? A cat."

Jeff is swinging past a slower moving car, cursing under his breath. She waits, only a moment.

"And how is Carla?"

"Busy with the goddamned ball. We had a big debate before going with this deb thing. Your granddaughter preferred to backpack in Europe. She's still planning on that."

"And Carla?"

Jeff's jaw muscles tighten. He whips into another lane.

"She's the one who wanted this for Allie, her last big stand as the all-caring mother, I suppose. I will say your daughter has done a good job in that department. They're close."

Close. Why does that sting? She's glad Carla is close to her own daughter, isn't she?

"That's good," she says, looking out at racing night traffic.

"You know this trip to Boston Carla made last month...."

"No. I don't know."

"Went up there to check out Harvard. What my wife plans to do with her academic notions, I couldn't tell you."

They've turned off the highway now to follow a tree-lined ribbon of road through enclaves of landscaped privacy, and now into a curving drive. Peg stares at the sprawling, two-story Colonial. *My daughter's house.* "The trees have grown," she murmurs, remembering a single Christmas here, Carla busy, Tracy in a ruffled bed piled with stuffed animals. Was that five years ago? No, seven?

The foyer in this serenely quiet house smells rich as they enter. Jeff nods for her to follow. The door is open to the readied guest bedroom. A bedside lamp glows on a mauve satin comforter. Jeff sets her bag down and brushes her cheek with his goodnight. In the silence of the elegant bath, she stands looking at herself . . . surprised not to see the image of an intruding ghost.

At breakfast Peg sits alone watching gardenias float in a silver bowl in this sun-streaked dining room. She feels like a visitor in a house on a *Southern Living* cover.

Granddaughter Tracy, a coltish seventeen, has offered a bright, moist face and quick kiss before rushing off to her own car and a swim party. Jeff has left too.

The housekeeper Hilda, a maternal blonde of Peg's generation, moves about as if she owns the place. Setting down a plate of hot croissants, Hilda pours coffee in the china cup, reporting cheerfully.

"They eat and run, all three of them. That's the way it is around here, but Lordy, it's been worse for the month. How about an omelet. No? Well, I'm glad Carla's Mama is here. At least these deb things and weddings get families together. I can remember when Christmas and grandma's birthday—or grandpa's funeral—meant homecomings and family reunions."

"Mother!" Carla walks in, willowy and fragrant in a peach silk robe, blonde hair lighter and longer than remembered. Peg jumps up, feeling shorter, smaller, a stranger to herself as they search each other's face for an instant before embracing.

The contact triggers a tremor of feeling, in her body, or Carla's, or both? A ringing phone ends the moment.

Hilda brings the portable phone to the table. Over the rim of her coffee cup, Peg watches her daughter deal patiently with the caterer. It's her chance to study this stranger, a part of herself lost to herself. My daughter, at forty, she thinks with a jolt of tenderness. The ivory skin seems tight over the finely boned face. Lashes nervous, hiding the pale green eyes as Carla deals with the problem of finger sandwiches. But this is Saturday. They have a week.

A memory flashes from where it has been lost. The image of a child at a back door, face aglow, holding up weed flowers for a gift. One perfect moment. Then another kind of memory. Carla, the inscrutable teenager, in some private trauma over a boy, allowing herself to be held for one trembling moment before pulling back, face controlled again, insisting, *"I'm all right"* when she wasn't. She'd walked out to a girlfriend's waiting car.

Carla hands Hilda the phone and turns back with a faint, tired smile.

"Mother, you look wonderful. You keep your same weight, don't you? Forgive me for not being up to greet you last night. I had another brutal headache. Hilda, don't we have strawberries? So! How do you like the house? I've redecorated since you've seen it."

It's the sound of a gracious hostess. Peg answers like the good guest.

"It's beautiful. You always had a sense of color and proportion."

"This deb business—you wouldn't believe how many details are involved in something you must think is frivolous. Of course it is. But it's over tonight. Now, about the week. . ." She pauses. Looks distressed. "Mother, I *had* planned for us to shop around Atlanta and do lunches."

Had? What happened to the week, the gift of the week?

"I'm afraid I have an interview in Boston on Monday. I thought it was coming up next week but it's now and I can't miss it. I've waited for this."

Waited, yes. "Boston," Peg manages to say. "Why Monday?"

"An interview with a department head about my credits. To find out if they'll accept me at Harvard for graduate work. In speech therapy. I've been interested in that for some time."

"I didn't know."

"It could mean two years' residence up there," Carla rushes on, looking past the table, the low bowl of gardenias, out to the garden beyond. "That is, if I'm accepted. So I have to go up—oh no, damn, the phone again."

The florist, this time. Carla listens and answers with smooth patience. Peg looks down at the huge strawberry on her plate, forks at it, and watches red pour onto the white china.

"Thank God all of this is over tonight." Carla hands the phone back to Hilda. "Mother, we'll have Sunday to catch our collective breath. And you must stay the week as planned. Hilda will look after you beautifully. You two can lunch and go to Rich's. Jeff and Allie take off in different directions by Sunday evening so you'll have the place all to yourself. Now, about today. . . ."

Today. And tonight, to be gotten through, public face intact.

". . . hair appointments for all of us," Carla is saying. "I want you to enjoy the shop, manicure, the works. They've blocked off the morning for the three of us. On the way over, you'll have to tell me how you are. Oh, and I must check with the hotel. We have a suite upstairs before the ball, for dressing and a reception. Cold buffet, sixty people. Christ, not the phone again—Hilda, catch it for me. I'm going up to dress."

Peg thinks every Atlanta florist must have backed up its van to the Hyatt Regency. Even the corridors are fragrant. Before the presentation hour begins in the flower-banked ballroom, the reception upstairs has the suite seething with silk and taffeta, formal black, and the pristine white gowns of a dozen debutantes. Voices set up an exuberant clamor. Granddaughter Tracy is a young beauty Peg doesn't know. Carla moves about, the efficient, serene hostess. Jeff expounds in a cluster of tuxedoed men.

In her long black silk gown and Carla's pearls, Peg stands holding her champagne glass, making mental notes, the kind she used to write, but now will take back to Luigi's.

She'll tell them about the young, clustered in their own groups, pretending amusement at this scripted charade—yet weren't they also enjoying this one night of bending to parents' tradition? At least bestowing dutiful but brilliant smiles to the balding uncles and parents' contemporaries moving in on their conversation. Their elders: slightly drunk on gin and tonic, and perhaps brief relief at tonight's generational truce. Grandfathers willing to ignore the earrings and ponytail hanging over a namesake's proper tuxedo collar. Grandmothers eager to believe the virginal white that shaped the young waists and billowed around restless satin slippers.

Now and again an animated Carla sweeps forward with someone in tow to say, "And this is my mother from Virginia."

Moving toward Peg now, a lanky boy in his formal gear, long blond hair tied back from a face that still looks like a teenager. He thrusts out a hand. "Tracy tells me you were a reporter once."

"Why, yes." Stories well up, things she can tell him. Names. Experiences. Encouragement. "Are you planning to go into journalism?"

"Right now I'm editor of the *Florida Alligator* at the University of Florida. I've interned the last two summers—*LA Times* first, then the *Washington Post*—so I have to make a choice before I graduate this fall."

Peg swallows back her stories. She feels a hundred years old, watching this kid move back into his crowd. Wait until she tells them back at Luigi's, *Not one but two generations have replaced us.*

Downstairs, the ballroom entrance is banked with blooms, the string orchestra playing *Memories*, chandeliers gleaming on family groups gathered for photographs. Peg wishes she could go over and help the harried photographer.

The presentations begin. From a sideline table now, Peg watches it happen beyond her own daughter's profile—the parade of debutantes in glistening white, red roses held close, one gloved hand on father's arm, father and daughter rounding the ballroom floor to the orchestra's romantic strains. Carla's face seems bright following Tracy and Jeff in that flowing tableau. So maybe this family is not splitting asunder as all signs indicate? *I had thought you were happy. I wanted you to be. But how could I know?*

Sunday is aftermath. The big house is silent, everyone sleeping late. Peg sits in the kitchen with Hilda, asking careful casual questions of the woman who must know everything about this household.

"This place is like a country club for Jeff's clients," Hilda says cheerfully, whipping up eggs for the omelets. "Carla and I run it that way, too. He's a big divorce lawyer you know, big on the women's side. They hang around the man. Jeff jokes about it, that's his way. I'm not telling tales.

Carla doesn't let it bother her, least she doesn't let on. That daughter of yours is a real gracious, with-it lady."

Hilda slides the golden omelet onto Peg's plate. "Now your daughter doesn't let anything keep her from giving Tracy attention. And she doesn't let that girl get away with what the other kids do. Rich kids around here are a spoiled bunch, believe me. They get too much, like some pay-off from parents. She's a good mother, I can vouch for that."

"I'm glad." Peg looks at her plate. "I was working when Carla was growing up. I don't know if she realizes that."

"She's mentioned you worked for a newspaper. Now this Boston thing—I guess you know she's been taking classes at Emory. Does her studying off by herself, doesn't talk about it. Being her mother, you can understand that. I can see she takes after you that way."

"Like me?" Peg puts down her fork to look at the bustling Hilda.

"Oh, I saw that right off. You both show a good face, but you deal with things inside without making a fuss about it. Not like those folks who groan and whine on talk shows. So I can't tell you what's going to happen here, and it's not for me to say. Maybe *they* don't know yet."

By afternoon, Hilda's information sits like a stone in the chest as Peg wanders through the handsome house, this showcase of false comfort. She picks up books and puts them down. Stands at the glass doors, gazing out to the gazebo and tennis court. Doubles going on out there. Lean, tanned young bodies playing to kill. In the shade of the court side bar, Jeff stands talking to two women, who sit with their backs to the bar, tanned legs crossed.

From the shaded pool patio Carla calls out in a lilting hostess voice, "Mother, come meet some people."

Peg does not want to meet more people. She wants to meet Carla. She waves at the people on the patio so as not to look rude. Back in the silent guest room, she leans back on the tufted spread and gives in to troubled sleep.

The sun is down when Peg repacks her suitcase and wanders out into the quiet house. Jeff and Tracy are gone. She knows Carla must be alone in the master bedroom.

In the wide arched doorway she watches her daughter standing by the bed in a posture of fatigue and uncertainty, wrapped in a white terry cloth robe, hair brushed loose, face pale without makeup. A blouse hangs limp in her hands.

"May I come in?"

Carla looks up. "There you are. Did Hilda look after you before she left? So much food left from the caterer."

Peg sits on the end of the large bed next to the opened suitcase.

"I'm fine." It's not true, but at this moment Carla looks too weary and vulnerable to hear anything else. "May I help? It's been quite a weekend. You look tired."

"Brain-tired. No, I don't need help, I'll be gone only five days. Your week here. And now you're leaving tomorrow—I'm really sorry, Mother." A faint smile, rueful or weary. "Are you still teaching people how to write up their lives?"

"Still have my class, yes. I didn't think you'd remember."

"Of course. My mother has always been busy." Carla tosses the blouse on the bed, stands looking down at it.

"After this past week, after last night, I can't even decide what to take."

Now, Peg thinks, *now, this moment, this last chance to say what's waited so long to be said.* Why shouldn't she let Carla know how she lies awake nights needing an honest, open conversation. How in a restaurant, or walking down a mall, minding her business, a jolt of loneliness can hit without warning at the sight of some mother and daughter walking along, talking together the way two women can do.

"Tomorrow. . . ." Carla sighs. "If you only knew—"

Peg waits, seeing what's behind the sigh. Concern about this Boston trip, about her present and future. Not the past.

Picking up the silk blouse, Peg spreads it on her lap, folds it carefully and places it in the case.

"Remember when I used to be the local Ann Landers? My responses were pretty good. To this day, check-out clerks still ask me questions. How about that? Do you want to talk . . . about anything?"

Carla stops pacing, voice a whisper. "You've seen this crazy household two days, so you know. Like Jeff, it demands—everything of me, all the time."

"Are you leaving Jeff? Carla, I didn't know you were unhappy. I wanted you to be happy—but you never told me."

"You never asked. You're so strong and confident. You expect everyone else to be."

"Do I? I didn't ask because I didn't want to intrude."

"What good, really, would it have done to tell you, Mother? There were times . . . when it was working. And times I knew I had to wait. Tracy will be in college by fall. Now it's my time to do what I have to do. Before it's too late."

"You waited for Tracy's sake."

"It's a choice I made. You always made your own choices, did what you felt you had to do. For you it was make a living, meet those deadlines." With a wry smile, "Remember my high school graduation?"

For a moment Peg doesn't remember. Then, "I think they were firing the police chief that night. I never made it to the auditorium, did I? I must have thought I had to cover that story." *I could still tell her how it was then, how it is now.* Only Carla is pacing.

"Do you know I worried what you would think, coming here this time, finding out I am risking this so-called comfortable life, something you never had. I wondered if you could understand."

Understand? "I know all about choices. They're always costly one way or another. But they're necessary. This Harvard plan, what counts is—does it feel right?"

"Oh yes. I have to try. I had hoped you'd understand and give the idea your blessing, but I didn't know what to expect. You are such a private person...."

"Carla—" Here's the moment again. Time for confirmation, justification. No. It's time to do what feels right.

Peg stands up, reaches out, pulls Carla to her, holds her seconds enough to feel her surprise become acceptance, warmth, and an answering hug.

Letting go, stepping back, Peg touches Carla's face, sees glistening eyes. "I'm so private? That makes two of us, daughter. I've used mine for protection. And you too? Ah, but we feel, don't we. Look, we can laugh and cry at the same time, right?"

"I was afraid you wouldn't understand."

"Get packing," Peg says. "I'm going to bed. I'm flying tomorrow. I do have a reason to get back. Truly."

Carla drops to the bed, flings herself back, arms outspread, with the abandon of a kid exulting that school is out.

"That damn ball. At last the thing's accomplished and behind me. But it was beautiful, don't you think? Writing a dissertation won't be as tiring."

"Pack and get some sleep. I'm ready to do the same."

"You sound like someone's Mama ordering the kid to bed." Carla, still stretched on the bed, yawning,

"Well, I am. Yours. Remember that."

"On the way to the airport tomorrow, I can tell you about my plans."

Carla's plans. No questions about her own reason to fly back home. "I'd like that," Peg says, "That's what I came to hear."

On Monday evening the rain-wet street gleams with the red neon of Luigi's Italian Villa. Peg walks in, looking for Binki and Tucker. The round table is as lively as a regular Friday night gathering. There's Tucker, Nina, Johnny, Elizabeth and Patrick. The whole ornery, loyal gang. And yes, Binki is there, wearing a funny golfing hat on his bald head.

He jumps up, reaches for her hand and pulls her into the circle.

"Glad you got your skinny little butt here. We're celebrating." His thin hand shakes, pouring red wine in her glass.

Peg doesn't know if they're celebrating Binki's good news or his stubborn refusal to believe the bad news. They all sound slightly tipsy.

"Well, what's the story?" Nina asks. "That was a quick family reunion. What happened?"

Their familiar faces wait. They really want to know. It's a gift, their caring to know.

"Reunions are different these days. So are families."

"Level with us," Nina says. "The report."

Some other time. Some other time when they are into one of their life and death discussions she will tell them more, tell them about the freedom that comes with letting go of old demands. For now this is Binki's night.

"I found a weekend is long enough to stand on the sidelines looking at other people's lives. Even your children's. Especially when they're in the throes of moving past forty. Lord, remember that time? You think your whole credibility is at stake unless you make it by tomorrow. Remember?"

Around the table, a chorus of agreements and groans.

"I saw my daughter off to Boston and Harvard. I wished her well, we did the hugs-and-kisses thing at the airport and I came home—to eat lasagna with fellow survivors of our own wars."

"Let's hear it for homecomings!" Binki says, sloshing around refills of Luigi's red wine. With irreverent toasts, they raise glasses, then click and clink around and across the table.

Bushes

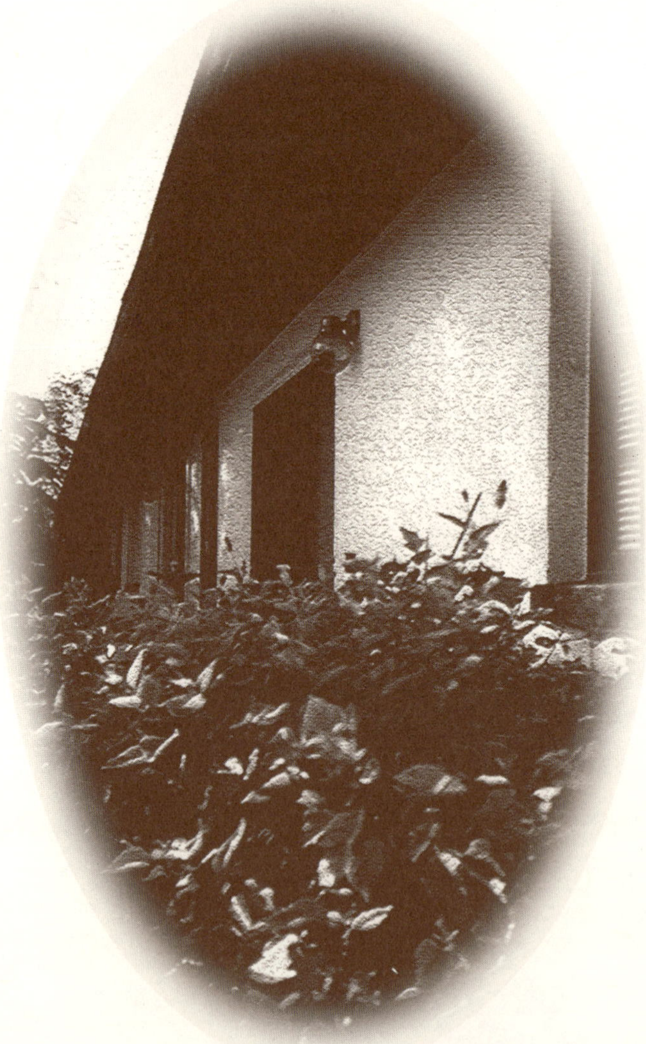

Bushes

The chain saw whined like a Grade B movie, fate coming closer. Too close now. Waking with a start, Libby bolted upright in bed, heart pounding under her nightgown.

The noise kept going right outside the bedroom, not five feet from her pillow. Some power-driven thing, droning and whacking away . . . *oh no* . . . at her hibiscus, the lush foliage against her window. An electric hedge trimmer was out there butchering, not trimming, her lovely bulwark of privacy, her filter of noise.

As branches fell, the sweaty face and working arms of a young man appeared, brandishing the noisy saw. Beyond him now stretched the condo complex's open center, with the clubhouse, a small ordinary clubhouse, sharing hot pavement with the pool, where other people's grandchildren whooped by day and strident neighbors bingoed or fussed at condo meetings by night.

Libby swung her legs out of bed and pulled on a robe as if she never had an energy problem and morning stiffness. In the living room, she opened the sliding glass doors and stepped out to her nine-by-seven pad of back door terrace, her own cloistered patio by virtue of head-high hibiscus and philodendron. Her cat Tommy watched at her ankles, his ears laid back at the buzzing noise.

There were three of them, sweating and hopping around with the electric trimmers, having a high old time mowing down her privacy, working ever closer to her patio. She shouted, "Stop this minute!" The motor shut off. "Who said you could cut down my bushes?"

The trio stalked over. They looked at her, then at each other. "Ma'am—that's what he told us to do. We're supposed to cut everything down below the windows."

"He?"

"The Colonel. Harold somebody. President of the Condo Association."

Libby never attended those noisy meetings, but knew enough about them from Belva next door. The president was a winter person from Chicago who didn't know the first thing about Florida foliage. Probably thought it was something you had to annihilate.

"I'm sure sorry, Ma'am," the crew leader spoke up, apologetic as if he had orders to kill her cat as well. "We've got to cut down all that by your back door, too."

"Don't you dare." She looked into their dutifully patient faces. It put her right back in front of one of her high school English classes. They were probably seeing her as just another skinny widow who lived behind these condo doors.

"Go tell that officious individual this resident says these branches do not reach the roof where they could do any possible harm. I keep everything trimmed below the gutters. Tell him this is my shade and my privacy and I don't want what's left to be butchered."

The yard crew shuffled their feet in the tangle of green branches. "Know how you feel," one said. "We'll hold off on your back door until you tell him that. But we've got orders, everything has to be down under the windows. We're supposed to finish the whole complex by tomorrow. Best we can do."

Libby went back inside and sat on the bed. The morning stiffness was there after all, as usual, but now it was mixed with new adrenaline. The hibiscus hedge was chopped to its bare roots below the bedroom window. She could look right out on bright open space, the dinky clubhouse and pool. The little flag was up, which meant a condo meeting tonight. It flew like a challenge.

What to do? She never went to those meetings. Surely not all the condo owners were willing for their bushes to be destroyed. Some had as fine shrubbery around their doors as her own, if not as high. With the exception of Belva next door, she didn't know other neighbors except to smile at anyone she met at the garbage bin or mail boxes.

There was of course the sweet-faced woman, Pearl, who lived across the court who had brought Tommy home in her arms more than once, saying, "I think he tries to visit me because he knows I would love to have a cat. But no, I can't. My husband is against it."

Listening for Belva to get home from her mall walking, Libby took her books on English castles and her tea out to the shaded patio as usual. But the pleasure wasn't there. This shade was about to be violated, too.

At her tap on the glass doors, Belva waved her in.

"Yeah, I heard them out there this morning. Sure, I knew it. Harold mentioned bush cutting last meeting.

He's the president. You should have been there to speak up. He's a blustery guy. You know how most of these men are, old retired military fellows or former bosses, they think they have to keep giving orders. That's the problem with most condo boards in Florida."

"But why does he want my foliage down?"

"The old bylaws say the landscaping should look uniform so Harold says that's how it should be. Besides, when the shrubbery is up past the windows, somebody could hide behind it at night, waiting to break in. He has a point there."

"Nobody but Tommy could hide behind mine. That's one of the reasons I want it there. For protection. As well as beauty. I didn't need blinds. I had this lovely leafy shade instead. Hasn't anyone protested?"

"One or two hands raised at the last meeting. Out of twenty-five sitting there like sheep. So Harold said, that's it. Everything will be cut."

"That's not Roberts Rules of Order. That's not the vote of everyone. I'm going to write a letter."

Belva shrugged. "Won't do a bit of good. You ought to show up and get involved." She gave Libby a level look. "Besides, that is, writing your letters to the newspaper about the state of the world you can't do anything about."

Miffed, Libby said, "I can explain my views much better on paper."

"I guess it's more comfortable speaking your piece that way. That's what they mean about ivory towers. Yours being behind your hibiscus. But if you want to save your patio shade, you'd better go to the meeting tonight and speak up. Fact is, your place is the one that has Harold teed off. He said it looks like a jungle on this side. Around your door, he means. Maybe you ought to know, Libby, they call you the woman who hides behind her bushes."

"Oh, for heaven's sakes." Belva's bluntness didn't offend her—when you knew people, you could take their opinions. But the news hurt.

"You mean they think I'm hiding from the world because I'd rather go to the library or stay home and work on my books about Britain than show up over there and play bingo?"

"Libby, I know how you spend your time, and why you save your money. For as long as I've known you, you've been planning that trip to England. Seven years? From all your reading, you should be able to lead tours yourself or drive the countryside like a native, left side of the street and all—if you ever really went."

Now she really felt peeved. "I've been waiting, until the right time." Until the airlines and the world got safer, she meant. Until she felt you could leave your place without somebody crawling in the window. And then there was Tommy who'd never be happy in a kennel cage.

Belva shrugged. "There's a meeting tonight and, if you want to keep your patio shade and privacy, you'd better show up and vote. I can't go because my daughter-in-law is calling about eight to see if I've found them a place to stay."

At seven-thirty, challenge humming in her pulse like trapped energy needing release, Libby marched across the flat stubble grass to the lighted clubroom. Three balding men sat at the head table, shuffling their papers. She walked in late, thirty or more assorted people already there, watching her arrival with curiosity. Thinking, she guessed, here's that weird woman who hides behind her bushes. Who to sit by? There, in the back, was the sweet-faced woman named Pearl who loved cats but couldn't have one because of the husband. They exchanged conspiratory smiles as Libby took the folding chair next to her.

"How is Tommy?" Pearl whispered, confiding, "I saw the most precious white Persian with green eyes in the pet store today. I go in just to look. Isn't that silly?"

Libby whispered back, "Not at all. By the way, what do you think about the shrubbery getting cut down today?"

Pearl shook her head and nodded toward the front table. "That's his idea. The one with the gavel, that's my husband. Harold has ulcers and when he sets his mind to something—"

The meeting began. Did anyone have anything to say about old business? Libby waved her arm and walked to the front, buoyed with purpose. Facing them, she used her pleasant but firm teacher's voice. "About the slaughtering of the shrubbery today—"

She had their full attention. Why, this felt better than writing letters to faceless editors.

"Some of you prefer a sterile look to your patios. That should be your choice. Some of us enjoy the beauty and protection of more lush plants around our back doors and windows. Harold here has taken upon himself to order all cut down. I protest. What do you think? Doesn't anyone want to speak up?"

Silence. Waiting, Libby raised her eyebrows higher. A florid-faced fellow growled from the back. "You chose to live in a condo, lady. That's the way it is. If the board votes we ought to have a uniform look, then that's what you get along with everybody else."

Holding on to her smile, "Yes, I did choose to live here. I love my apartment and my shady back patio. Isn't anyone here interested in beauty? In having your own mini-garden?"

"They've voted," another voice complained. "You have to bend to the rules. Fact of life in condos."

Libby rocked on her heels a minute. She wanted to remind them anyone who has lived sixty years has contended with the facts of life, knowing some of them get on record books as stupid, unfair, uncontested laws.

"Doesn't anyone want to protest this decision? Harold's decision?"

A few faces looked embarrassed for her. Silence. Harold banged his gavel, and announced, "Sell out and move if you don't like the rules."

She kept her voice calm. "I like to believe there are any number of choices in a situation. If this board insists on outlawing natural beauty around private doors, then I must make some additional choices."

"Is that a threat, lady?" A male guffawed from the back.

Harold banged the gavel. "Enough of this. It's decided. Rest of that shrubbery goes down tomorrow. Now if you've had your say—"

Libby did a little bow and wave, hoping it looked like aplomb. Out she walked, back across the grass to her back patio door. The new adrenaline still pumped in her pulse, demanding release by some action. Well, it would be by her own decision, not Harold's.

When the crew came next morning to whack away her remaining screen of privacy, Libby took out glasses of cold Coke.

"Go ahead, boys," she said to their apologetic faces. "My hibiscus must fall to uniform rules around here. My plants are victims. But I'm not."

The crew leader looked uncertain but sounded sympathetic. "We're pruning yours especially careful. Does shrubbery good, really." He grinned. "The Colonel, Harold, he doesn't realize this stuff will grow faster than ever. You folks should find somebody else easier to work with, who's willing to be on the board."

Belva slid open her glass doors before Libby had a chance to rap. "I heard about last night. You're not going to sell your place, are you? Why, look at you. I thought you'd be fuming mad this morning."

"I wouldn't think of selling. You've been wondering where to put your family for a month? Put them right here in my place. For free—if they'll feed Tommy and make sure he's in at night."

"Where in the world are you going?"

"You should know."

Three weeks later, in a little pub in Cambridge, England, Libby sat down to enjoy her mid-morning tea and pastry and to write Belva a letter.

"You should see outside the window right now. Old, winding street. Bicycles whizzing around little English cars. Down the street is King's College Chapel. Every morning I take a walk along the grassy banks—they call them the 'backs'—along the Cam, a river that's peaceful as a stream in a bucolic meadow."

"Ivy on these ancient colleges must be about as old as the stone and gargoyles. Old, but green. You know I love green. The grass and trees here, mint green. And the gardens in this soft English sun! Well, I hope you got to the condo meeting after I left. I want to hear all about it when I get home."

Libby sat back, fingering her afternoon tour bus ticket. Right now she wanted to imagine the condo meeting. That nice girl from the pet store had promised to show up in person with the white Persian kitten with the green eyes and present the surprise gift to Pearl "in appreciation of husband Harold's well-meaning service to the board, from Pearl's friend and neighbor who is at the present away, enjoying English gardens."

If Harold chose to be a heartless old bastard of a husband in front of everyone by refusing to let Pearl accept that kitten—well, that would be his choice. People remembered things like that. Regardless, board elections came up within two months. She was thinking seriously about running for office on a beautification agenda, to get some nice foliage around that tacky clubhouse. Yes.

"More tea, Luv?"

The ruddy faced young man had seen her lifted cup.

She smiled up at him. "No, I was making a private toast here." A slightly grudging toast to Harold, and to the benefits that could be found in the slings and arrows of outrageous fortune.

Moon Lady

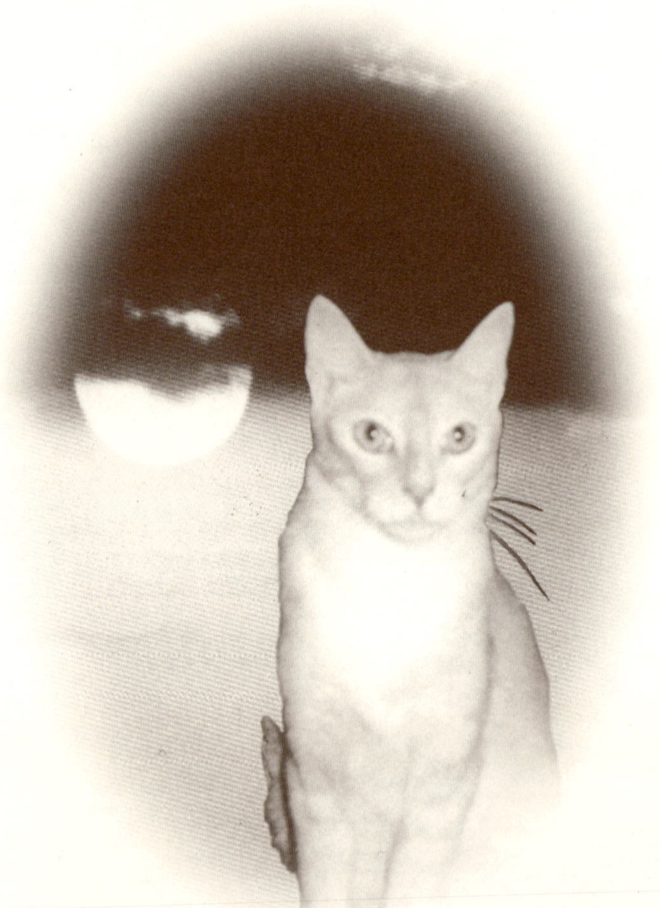

Moon Lady

My neighbor Molly McFee says what happened here at Harmony Gardens the last couple weeks is not weird fate. "Everything has a reason and sometimes it takes a while coming down, Vera Honey. Only it's not over. When two things happen like that, expect a third."

We were sitting on the stoop of her double-wide, everything looking back to normal, after two excitements I wouldn't want to live through again. My Robert was doing his homework next door in my single-wide. I said, "Well whatever it is—it's bound to mean more bad luck for me."

"Honey, you're young, and haven't found this out yet. But I'm telling you. It's not about luck. Expecting the worst can make the worst show up. You look for the best and help make it happen."

The first time Molly tried to tell me that was right after I'd moved into Harmony Gardens. Before I met her, on my second night there, already I was thinking—*Way to go, Vera, you've made another mistake.*

Three weeks before, driving past, I'd spotted Harmony Gardens with its mobile homes tucked back off the highway under big old oaks, little sandy roads running through.

You'd have thought all of these old-time Florida trailer parks had been wiped away by now for high rise condos and doctor offices, but here was one the bulldozers had missed. I figured living inside that nice shade had to be a heck of a lot better than where I was, in a tacky duplex on the street full of mean kids. Robert could ride his bike under those trees after school without bigger boys scaring him back inside.

At the next corner, spur of the moment, I wheeled around and drove back and parked in front of the office, the single-wide facing the road. Inside, a glum acting fellow, feet up, watching TV, looked me over. Wanted to know if I had a job.

Yes, and I also have a ten-year-old son, I told him right off. He grumbled but I stood right there telling him Robert was a real quiet kid. There wasn't any need to explain Robert is quiet because he's so insecure about being overweight. He likes doing his homework with Twinkies. I'm just glad he does the homework.

The man—he was the owner, Tomkins—shrugged and said 8-G was available. I said fine and put down a month's rent right there.

It was available, all right, and full of mildew and palmetto bugs. The second afternoon I came home from work with sprays and groceries, Robert was slumped in the tiny living room, sniffling. The woman across the path with the bushy red hair had given him the "evil eye" and delivered warnings. Folks wouldn't put up with a bicycle coming up behind them, and he'd better not leave it lying around for someone to fall over, either.

In the laundry room, I realized Harmony Gardens had as much harmony as my job behind the Customer Service desk at Super Discount. I should have known—a park like this, filled with old biddies who have nothing to do but watch the soaps, tend to each other's business and complain how they should be living somewhere else. They looked me over like disapproving aunts, while I pulled wet laundry out of a rusty washer and stuffed it into a creaking dryer.

Just as well I didn't have a boyfriend at the present. Coming in here he'd feel like an insect under a magnifying glass.

The evil-eye lady—Mrs. Eva Belwether—let me know the park never gets any improvements because Tomkins, the owner, hates Harmony Gardens. Calls it a boa constrictor on his back. Sits in that office down on the front road reading travel magazines and taking gulps of Mylanta. His taxes have gone up, but he can't raise the rents or "we'd all move out."

Those old gals really enjoyed telling me Tomkins' troubles. How he can't sell because his sister owns one-half the property and the two of them don't speak. The sister lives in the family home next to the park, in a big two-story set back from the road. It's over there, hidden by overgrown bushes, pines and oaks.

Mrs. Belwether looked smug and disapproving all at once. "We see the airport limo taking her off to one place or another all the time. We hear she goes on these fancy cruises. To spite Tomkins, I'd say."

Besides the gossip, they had advice and warnings. If I saw a face leering out of old Mrs. Hunnicutt's double-wide, that would be her son, Leland, who wasn't "right." I was supposed to hurry on by and "don't look him in the eye."

Eva Belwether shrugged her big shoulders warning me about Molly McFee. "The one in the double-wide next to you. She's batty. Has to be. Sits out on the stoop every night with her cat, like she's communing with the moon."

A birdlike lady, clicking her teeth added, "That woman does her laundry late at night when everybody else is inside watching TV. Early mornings, she walks the whole park three times, does something to her flower beds, then goes inside until the moon comes out. Doesn't even own a TV."

Eva Belwether said, "You'd think she was a witch in disguise, living amongst us. Talking to that cat. Doing some kind of spell on her petunias to have them grow like that with hardly any sun."

Every other yard in Harmony Gardens has Florida sand spurs. No missing that fact.

Second night, when I came out for a breath of air, Molly McFee called me over, cheerful as you please. She turned out to be a little round woman with a cap of short white curls, sitting on her front stoop in the shadows. After a rough day at Super Discount, I was feeling so low, I needed company and didn't care if she was a little batty.

We sat there eating fine lemon cake on a napkin, her cat Nalo nosing around, and telling me how glad she is to have a young neighbor. "Don't you love a moonlight night? Look at those patterns the trees make. What's your name?"

"Vera—Vera Russo." The Russo was because I'd married a big chested Italian who took off before Robert was one-year-old. Looking down at her petunias in the moonlight, I had to ask how she got them to grow like that in this sandy place?

"Honey, I just treat them the way petunias like to be treated."

I found myself telling her about my awful job and about Robert being so insecure.

"Then you can be thinking about what kind of job you do want instead. Have to do that before it happens."

I just smiled. Then here came a bike rider through who must not think Molly was batty because he stopped to talk as if this was a regular thing. A nice looking long legged fellow, lanky and silver haired, the way Gregory Peck looks now.

"Mr. Paulson, you got yourself a fine night for pedaling. This pretty young woman here is Vera, my new neighbor, I'm happy to say. If you and Mrs. Paulson still had your restaurant she'd be just right as a greeting hostess, don't you think? And how's Mrs. Paulson?"

"Face in her cards," he said, with a smile, as if that was a joke between them. When he pedaled away, Molly explained. Mr. Paulson and his wife live in the fancy high rise down the road. They used to own a big restaurant in Chicago before retiring down here in Florida. Now all they do is go out to dinner. Rest of the time Mrs. Paulson plays solitaire. Nights he rides his bike through here, very respectfully, waving back when anybody stares.

"Mrs. Paulson needs to get busy again," Molly said, "but she concentrates on being bored."

"What about the busy-bodies I meet in the laundry room?"

"Oh, they enjoy fussing about this place, can't you tell. Not that it's any fun to listen to. They just love to threaten Tomkins they'll move."

The first three weeks at Harmony Gardens everything went on as usual, me visiting with Molly, when I wasn't down at the laundry having to listen to gossip. The one night I had a date, I left from the store and Molly brought soup over to Robert for supper. I sure needed a friend like that even if she was more than twice my age, living on Social Security and a nurse's pension.

The next night, I told Molly about the date. "No more. He was a first class jerk. There goes my social life again into the pits. Now you're going to tell me I had bad expectations."

"No, maybe you were just smarter sooner. Saved yourself wasting any more time. Vera Honey, how you doing with the laundry room ladies? I know they think I'm strange, watching the moon instead of television."

"Why would they think that?" I asked, trying to be polite. We were sitting out in the humid night catching a breeze. Now and then it was cool and sweet, then a whiff of somebody's supper.

Molly sighed. "For some people, anything is strange if it's opposite to whatever belief they're stuck in. They can't understand why I'm not complaining about living here. I have better things to do."

"What's that?" Because I had been wondering.

"Studying up on how to run an English tearoom once I get one."

Oh my. First I'd heard about that. "Where did you get such an idea?"

"I did a jig-saw puzzle one time, way back, a million pieces it seemed, picture of Ann Hathaway's cottage in England. I was eighteen I guess, in nursing school. I knew I had to get there and see the real thing. And someday have an English-looking tearoom with flowers in front."

"Did you ever get there?"

"Oh, yes. When you dream a thing good enough and put out the right kind of energy, it does open the door to letting it happen."

"I've wished for plenty and I've always gotten the opposite." I told her, patting Nalo sitting there like a cream-colored ghost cat between us.

"Like what, Vera Honey? What have you wished for?"

"A husband who didn't run away from being a father. But I knew from the first he might be that kind, to say cheerio, Babe, once he had responsibilities. Guess I fell for those big shoulders."

"You hear that, Vera? You have hopes and fears mixed in together. Won't work that way. What else do you wish for right now?"

"Well, I'd like a really good job where I could dress nice and greet people with a smile and not 'what's your complaint?' So tell me—did you really get to England?"

"Eventually," Molly said, in a dreamy way. "When I was forty. I had a hospital patient who needed a nurse to go with him, back home to London. Well I quit my job and went. I had two days left over to take a tour bus to see Ann Hathaway's cottage. Been planning to make mine look something like that ever since. I have a shelf of books inside. I'll be ready once I get the place to do it."

It popped out of my mouth. "And here you are renting a double-wide in Harmony Gardens." I looked quick at her round face in the shadowed night, hoping I hadn't hurt her feelings.

But no, Molly sounded confident as ever, saying, "For now, I'm enjoying arranging it in my mind. The details can always be worked out later, when the opportunity opens up."

The very next day the first excitement happened at Harmony Gardens and it sure didn't have anything to do with Molly getting an English tea room.

It started with Robert leaving his bicycle in the wrong place, lying flat between our front stoops. So guess who fell over it? My only friend in Harmony Gardens, Molly McFee. She was headed home after leaving us a bowl of potato salad. With no moon, she tripped on the bike and must have flown through the air to come down on her head. Fell into her petunia beds, short of the steps.

I heard the *eekkkk,* and ran out to see Molly stretched out on her back in her flowers. Just then Mr. Paulson came wheeling around the bend, as he does every night, but fast this time, because he must have heard the *eeekkk.* Propped his bike against a tree and bent over her same time I got there. Molly was really out of it. She seemed to be smiling up at the night. Mr. Paulson pulled out his cell phone and dialed 911. Robert had run back in. I could hear him bawling.

An emergency rescue van came sirening off the highway, weaving around the sandy curves, looking for a knocked-out little woman lying in a petunia bed. People spilled out to stand around, gawking. Real sirens must be one sure thing to get them away from the ones on TV.

Someone croaked out loud, "Most excitement we've had since Leland got the knife after his mother."

I wanted to ride in the emergency van to the hospital, but there was Robert in the house, scared to death and crying. The crowd watched as the van made its way out. In the shadows, their faces looked the way faces can do, wide eyed, enjoying watching something real happen.

Next morning I called the hospital hoping for the best. My fears must have been stronger. Molly McFee was still unconscious.

The second morning I demanded the day off. Almost cost me the lousy job, but the manager said a grudging okay, since it was my only aunt who may be dying. At the hospital, I caught the doctor in the hall and said I was her only relative. He gave me a funny look. Told me Molly had been unconscious for six hours but all vital signs were good. The concussion was mild. A broken collar bone seemed to be the only injury and she was awake.

"However, she is having delusions. Probably temporary," he said stiffly. "Your aunt must have read stories about people who thought they were floating on the ceiling."

I wanted to say, but didn't, well Buster, why does that make you so indignant? You're a doctor and shouldn't jump to conclusions like the old gals at Harmony Gardens.

I went in to find Molly propped up in her high bed, looking bright-eyed and peaceful. "Vera Honey!" She opened her arms to hug me as though falling over Robert's bicycle had been a good thing.

"That poor man," she said, meaning the doctor. "I unsettled him no end. I only told him he thought he was getting his ulcer back, but it was really the argument with his daughter, something about her college. Or maybe he didn't like me telling him what was going on when they were trying to wake me up. He shouldn't have spoken to the nurse that way. Oh, here I am talking about myself when you had such a time getting time off from your job."

"How did you know that?"

"Pull up that chair and visit. And look at those yellow roses in the window. Came from the Paulsons. See how the sun and petals are reacting to each other? I watched all morning. They're saying something to me."

I thought, *Oh my, Molly McFee, you really have gone off your rocker.*

"Don't think I've gone off my rocker," she said, quick as that. "I can't explain it, but I just know, like I knew the doctor's stomach is fighting with his head. Oh honey, don't frown so. And you tell Robert, my head must have needed to get shook-up because these things flash in my mind clear as a stop light, flashing *Wait* or *Walk Now*."

Molly came home looking like her old self, except she was more quiet, as if listening to the messages in her head. So I believed it when she said one night, with a sigh, "Something's about to happen, Vera."

"More sirens in the park?"

"Could be," she said, gazing into the night.

"You're expecting something bad—the way you tell me not to do?"

"Don't know. It can come down either way."

Two evenings later, when I turned off the road into Harmony Gardens, a police cruiser followed me in. Two more were already parked in front of my single-wide and three or four cops were ordering bunches of neighbors to get back. I about had a conniption. Left my Camaro in the sand spurs and ran toward my place. Oh Lord, something must be happening to Robert.

A police officer was shouting toward my screen door, "Leland Hunnicutt, you come out now and nobody's going to hurt you." He grabbed me by the wrist before I could run in. "You the mother? Stay out. We'll handle this."

Leland, the fellow you weren't supposed to notice in his mama's window, the one who chased his mother with a knife, was inside with my Robert. Somebody in the crowd called out, "Molly McFee's in there, too. Been in there thirty minutes."

I screamed a squeaky soprano, "Molly—Robert—what's going on?"

Here came Mrs. Hunnicutt, barreling through the watchers, screaming at the top of her lungs like some heroine in an old movie. "Leland, baby, you come out to Mama. Don't you hurt nobody. *Leland!* You hear what I say?"

Molly appeared at the door, motioning to the policeman below my stoop. He went up to the door, hand on his holster. Everything went quiet. Molly must have been doing the talking because the policeman was standing there, glowering, rocking on his heels.

They kept on talking through the screen door, everybody so dead quiet I could hear my heart roaring in my ears. The officer turned and walked back to his cruiser, leaned in to talk on the radio that squawked back. Then he talked to the other two cops, before he turned to the crowd of gawking neighbors.

"Everybody go home," he ordered. "You too, Mrs. Hunnicutt. We'll talk to you later. Everything's under control. I mean it, everybody go home." He barked it out, though he didn't look too sure. I was in a worse state than Leland's mother only I wasn't being melodramatic about it and waving my arms.

I stood there numb, watching the crowd back away, mumbling, Mrs. Belwether pulling Mrs. Hunnicutt along. The officer put his arm around me—I had to grit my teeth not to burst into tears by then—because he was telling me, "Your boy's all right, Ma'am. But you wait here." He went to his cruiser and talked some more into the radio. The two other cruisers rolled on by, shooing people who were taking their time, still looking back.

It was too quiet now as the officer went back up my stoop and opened the door. Out came Molly with her arm around Leland, a gangling, a boney-looking fellow about twenty, lank hair hanging by his scared face. You'd have thought Molly was introducing her friend Leland to the flustered looking cop, who nodded and nodded, as he talked to Leland. All I made out was, "Miss Molly here was right, you'll like where you're going."

I ran inside. Robert was at the kitchen table stuffing lemon cake in his mouth, looking wide-eyed.

"What happened?" I squeaked.

"That was old crazy Leland. Only he's not really crazy. He thinks he has to scare people with a knife. But Molly explained to him—gee, I forgot what all she said. I was hiding in the corner at first."

Molly must have ridden away with Leland and the policeman so I didn't get the rest of it until hours later, when a cruiser brought her home. I was waiting on her front stoop.

"That poor boy," she said, sitting down heavily. "He's slow, but he's not crazy. His mother keeps him hiding like a poor animal afraid of everybody. He thinks he's a freak because no one will look him in the face. Thinks waving around a knife makes people look at him with respect. Got the idea way back, watching TV. I went over there with the cake and there was Robert crouched in a corner and Leland waving the knife from your sink."

I moaned. "Now Robert will really be afraid the rest of his life."

"No, you don't want that, Vera Honey. And Robert doesn't either. He saw what being afraid did to Leland."

"So tell me."

"I saw Leland was waving that kitchen knife with such a frightened face, I knew clear as anything, he had some fear besides trouble with his mother. I do get messages, like a flash, since that fall. Just don't tell anybody. Anyway, it came to me, and I said, 'Leland, nobody minds your ears but you.' He stared at me, clapped his hands over his ears, and dropped the knife. I picked it up wiped it off and started cutting the cake I'd brought over. I fixed them two plates. Robert was in the corner. I'm sure thankful he came over and sat down, too."

Chin in her hands, Molly sighed. "I looked them both straight in the eye and said, while you boys sit here and eat your cake, I have something good to tell Leland. You see, Vera Honey, I knew about the home the social services people wanted to take him to that other time he waved the knife at his mother. Mrs. Hunnicutt put up such a fuss, that worker just left and didn't look into the case any more. Guess they have enough on their hands."

I sat there listening.

"So I told Leland he was twenty-one now he could choose to go to this boarding school and get training for a job and have spending money and friends, too. Told him he didn't have to live with his mama and be ashamed of himself, in fact his mama would be proud of him later. I went on like that—but it was all true."

Molly rubbed her forehead. "I have to go in now. I'm awful tired out."

I hugged her goodnight. I hugged Robert, too, at home, and told him how proud I was he was so brave. He swaggered a bit and told me, "I sure don't want to be like Leland."

For two days, I didn't get to talk with Molly. Once I saw her little old VW up by Tomkins office. Usually it stayed parked against her double-wide. I waited on her stoop until she rolled up. "Why, Vera, what's up?"

"You tell me," I said. "I have the feeling this third thing is going to come down and you know what it is."

"Gracious me. I'm not sure. I'm busy though, putting out some positive energy. That's all you can do."

That was all the explanation I was about to get. One week after that business with Leland, Tomkins drove through in a strange car with a loud speaker on top. He sounded excited and official, barking out for everyone to meet up by the office at eleven the next morning. There would be free hotdogs and an announcement.

Eva Belwether and the others stood on the sandy road, talking and wondering. Tomkins had never offered free hotdogs before, not even on any July Fourth.

I had to go to work next day so I knocked on Molly's front door soon as I got home. "What's happening?"

She asked me into the living room. "Sit down, Honey, and I'll tell you, only don't let those folks get it out of you. Tomkins wants to announce it himself. He and his sister are selling the whole place to Mr. and Mrs. Paulson."

"Weird! How did that happen? What kind of magic did you put out?"

"Not magic, but energy, like I said. You don't sit back and just hope, you put out energy too. First, I knew Tompkins' sister has been home for awhile, and must be in the big house all by herself, lonely. Then I went to see Tomkins."

She looked pleased.

"I said, you know, you could go over there and talk about the home place, about growing up there and how Harmony Gardens is going down, a disgrace to the family memories. I left him with the idea. Then I went to see the Paulsons and said, bet you could talk those two old siblings into selling these beautiful six acres, seven counting the house. Nothing as pretty like it anywhere left with a sale sign on it."

I had to ask, "What would they want with a bunch of old run down mobile homes and complaining renters?"

"True, true. But Mr. Paulson always did dream about building a new restaurant so he and Mrs. Paulson can be happy and busy again. He's even been looking for property, thinking he was just playing with the idea. My mind picked up on that. He loves this place. Now he's going to buy it. Already planning how he'll keep most of the oaks and use a lot of glass."

"What about the people here?" I didn't say—and what about me?

"The realtor who's been looking out for Mr. Paulson is going to help them settle in an apartment complex he's handling. It's newer with some puny pines."

"Not that they really wanted to move," I said. That went for me too.

"Honey, they'll get what they claimed they wanted—to move out."

"Where does that leave me and Robert? And you, Molly. I don't think you want to live in some little old tight complex."

"You are right about that. The sister is going to move in the high rise where the Paulsons are. I figured she'd like something high and fancy for when she's not on her cruises." Molly's round face was beaming. "The old Tomkins home place? Going to be a big gift shop. Fancy Florida restaurants have to have gift shops, right?"

"And you—?"

"I've offered to do the flower beds and give it a lived-in look."

"You're going to *live* there? Don't tell me you're going to have yourself an English tea shop."

"Old Florida, English-flavored maybe. Along with the gifty rooms. A place for people to wait or lollygag around before going down a pretty path to dinner."

I sat there not able to say a thing, but behind my closed eyes I was seeing myself dressed pretty, greeting people at the door, or maybe over in the Paulsons' restaurant, with its glass walls looking out on old oaks and the intercom saying *Party 273, your table is waiting.* When I opened my eyes, Molly was beaming.

I guess she read my mind all right, because she said, "That's right, Honey."

Marian Coe

Waiting at the Matterhorn

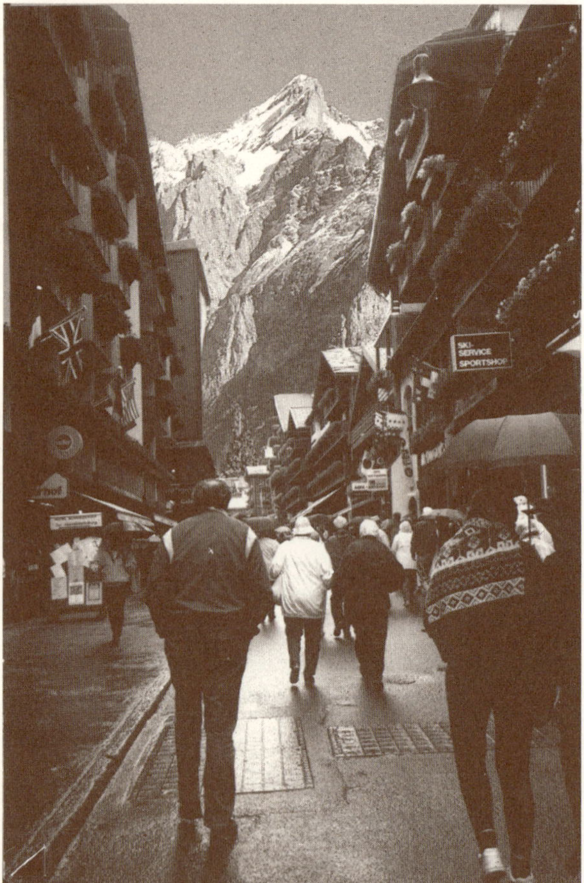
SKI-
SERVICE
SPORTSHOP

Waiting at the Matterhorn

When Robin gave up on getting *Steven to a Couples Renewal Retreat, she signed herself up for a class in Solving Problems through Creative Visualization.*

First night, floor-sitting with six strangers, pillows to lean on, and charged with sharing, Robin made her reasons sound funny—at least not desperate. Yes, she would be visualizing for a way to get her husband out of his office and away from his laptop computer long enough to . . . well, connect, talk again like two people, not as Mr. Perfectionist lecturing to Mrs. Dreamer.

Five faces did not look amused. The frizzy haired woman who reminded Robin too much of her mother murmured something about anal-retentive, self-righteous males and why didn't she leave the stiff?

Robin folded her arms and clamped her lips in a cold, polite smile. She wasn't going to give up on four years of marriage and end up like her mother, living now in California with a fifth husband.

By the third night of guided meditation, and silence, with flute music drifting past like freed-thought, Robin came up with her possible solution.

"You did *what?*" Steven looked up from the brochure with his CPA frown, the one he used on clients who brought in messy records for the IRS. "You've already booked this without any discussion? A trip calls for planning."

"Booked and paid for it," Robin said, as if she didn't notice the indignant shock. "Don't worry. I used the you-know-what account." Her mother had been sending checks for the past few Christmases and birthdays like a substitute for communication. Apparently the current husband in California was rich. Robin had watched the checks mount, but hadn't touched the account. Until now for this necessary cause. Steven sat there, frowning at the brochure, so Robin prompted, "Imagine, traveling through all the Alpine Countries. And Germany."

If she'd bought a week at one of those Jamaican resorts like Sandals, with the brochure showing couples living it up over drinks against tropical sunsets, he would have known what she was doing. But hadn't he always talked about his grandparents coming from Germany and Austria and how he'd visit there someday? And since she'd been a kid back in Georgia, reading *Heidi,* she dreamed of being in those Swiss Alps, eating cheese and crusty bread, looking out on all that scenery.

Switzerland had to be a place where a person could feast the soul, even from a bus window. No window in Cleveland had ever afforded that kind of thrill.

Steven ran a thoughtful hand over his close cropped blond head. "Why a bus tour? And leaving in three months?"

"Because everything's already organized on a bus tour. You can write that cousin you have in Germany. Maybe get to meet him." She knew not to say a word about making love under strange covers.

When he started complaining about leaving the office all of eighteen days, counting travel, Robin said, "That Ruth person you have in there now,"—she didn't say that officious woman in your office—"you've said how well she could run things." Seeing his nod, Robin knew to stop talking and start hoping. Something was going to happen to change everything and she couldn't wait.

Globus Tour. Alpine Countries, Day 2: ARRIVAL IN FRANKFURT, GERMANY after your transatlantic flight. Time to rest or explore the bustling metropolis and beautifully restored Romerberg Square. . . . Tonight you'll meet your traveling companions. . . .

Sleepy as she is, Robin's spirit soars as the Delta banks for the landing. Big mistake, taking that sleeping pill at 4 p.m. when they took off out of New York. The pill hadn't worked. Too much going on in the plane with the movie and all. Steven had said, "Just put your mind to it," then to prove it, tucked the pillow under his neck and went to sleep. Or pretended to. Robin watched until he really was asleep. He could look so sweet when that little frown between his eyebrows relaxed, his cropped blond hair popping up in curls against the pillow.

Landing now. Goosebumps. She rubs Steven's arm. "Don't you feel something wonderful is about to happen?"

"Besides riding a bus with assorted people for 15 days?"

Okay, she won't talk about expectations again. Will keep it to herself, where she always keeps her hopes. It'll happen, though. It feels sure as a premonition now. She has to wait and let it happen.

In the huge, bustling Frankfort terminal, Steven is over at the bank windows, exchanging money, using his German. Robin could stretch right out on the cold floor and sleep, red Globus bag as a pillow, but no. The itinerary says: *Your Alpine Tour starts today!*—so someone should be racing up any minute talking in exclamation points about "15 glorious days." She makes herself sit up, eyes stretched open, waiting to be collected.

A trim fellow does rush up, looking harried. He's Werner, the tour director. "You the Irving Meyers, New York? No? You are the Steven Harpers, Cleveland. Vait here. I must find the others. I haf to learn forty new faces every two veeks." And off he goes.

On the bus to the Ramada, Steven is wide awake, into conversation with a fellow across the aisle who says he's in insurance in Omaha. She leans against the window watching the "bustling metropolis" roll past, like so many gray postcards going out of focus. But glory, their hotel room will have a bed and there'll be three hours before going downstairs to "meet the traveling companions."

Day 3: FRANKFURT-MUNICH. Today is dedicated to Germany's Romantic Road leading from the flat country

toward the Alps. We'll spend time in spectacular Rothenburg with its cobbled lanes and ramparts, on to lovely medieval Nordlingen. . . . Tonight, the Hofbrauhaus in Munich. . . .

Everyone piles back on the bus after walking around Rothenburg taking pictures and buying postcards. Standing up front with the mike, Werner starts telling them about the ride toward Danube Valley into Munich and how they'll be rotating seats every day.

Robin gets out her new trip diary. This will be like writing a story as it happens, without knowing how it will end.

Diary: Rothenburg really is a walled city with 16th century houses. Now I know where Disney people get their ideas; they come to places like this and copy the real thing. My feet are tender from walking on cobblestones. Shouldn't have brought these shoes.

She looks up with a brief attentive smile for Werner, lecturing away at the mike.

Our tour guide, Werner, doesn't look so worried this morning now that he has the tour going. Has even told us a bit about himself. He's never been to the U.S. He's Austrian. Loves the German poet-philosopher Goethe. Says: "When I was in school I had to read sousands of pages of Goethe. No one in the world with such an IQ." Just love the way he talks.

Steven by the window is engrossed in the passing scenery. A good sign. Should she put that down? He won't be reading what she writes.

She closes the dairy for now, leans back against the humming seat. Beyond the dark curly head of the Italian driver, his big shoulders bent in stoic concentration over the steering wheel, the road ahead streams under the huge bus. It would be really interesting to talk to him at some stop, when he's standing around alone, smoking, only he doesn't speak English, and when she tried this morning, he just shook his head, jet-dark eyes telling nothing. She imagines him walking in on his lover, wherever she is, sweeping her in his arms, falling into bed and laughing in her ear about this new load of Americans, and working again with nervous Werner.

She should make notes on these "traveling companions." since they're part of this trip story, whatever it turns out to be. From the looks of the one she talked to, or watched during last night's dinner, Steven can't suspect she's brought him here for any reason other than see where his grandfather came from.

Diary: Notes on this tour bunch:

Retiree couples, more than half the crowd. Last night they were in high spirits, all right; plunged right in telling about other trips they've taken.

Maybe Steven would notice a couple, even looking mismatched, can enjoy being with each other in their own way, even after thirty, forty years?

The Florida Couple, interesting, maybe they'll be friends on this trip. Ron Neeley and Joan. Younger than the other retirees.

The Neeleys make her think of a bride and groom from the top of a white cake, who had aged just enough to turn his sideburns silver, and change her light brown to a good beauty salon blonde. Two neat looking people, still loving enough to touch and smile and whisper to each other.

She'd sat with them at dinner, when Steven got himself involved again with the bald-headed insurance fellow from Omaha. The insurance wife waved Robin over to join them but Steven didn't look up, so she waved back and stayed with the Neeleys who were sharing impressions and not boasting about any kids back home.

The Oregon Sisters. All four look like they're past caring about what to wear on a trip yet all fired up to see the alpine countries. Olga, the one with bushy gray perm, even uses a walking cane.

The four seemed so happy traveling together, Robin dubbed them the Oregon Sisters, though Joan Neeley said they were members of the same travel club back home.

The Traveling Family, an energetic ruddy-faced husband, a matching wife and his ninety-year-old father, Barney, who looks like he can keep up with them.

Robin gives her attention again to Werner talking about Munich being as beautiful as Paris. He sits down and she goes back to her diary.

Chelsea, a lanky English girl about my age, all over the dining room last night, talking Italian with the waiters, stopping by a table of retiree couples, breezing on to the next. Wears crazy long skirts, weird-looking sweaters like someone who doesn't care what anyone else thinks.

Joan Neeley had filled her in on Chelsea. "Interesting young woman. I would guess she buys her clothes in the Camden Market or the bohemian stalls I've seen on Portobello Road in London. Even the rich will dress that way, you know, at least the young. I gather the older woman with her, the one in the black suit, was once her English Nanny."

Ron Neeley added: "Chelsea hasn't been around us, Robin, so we must not be prospects for whatever she's buzzing the others for."

Diary: And now for the most curious couple on this tour: Mrs. Eldridge from Tennessee and that awful glum fellow traveling with her.

Last night, Mrs. Eldridge's entrance caused a lot of suppressed smiles. A tall skinny woman, she trailed in wearing a black slinky dress, fringed orange shawl tossed over her bony shoulders, hair swirled on top of her head, dyed too black for her white face. The silver-topped walking stick might have been part of her costume, or a wand to poke underlings into action. She came in looking over the humming room from under high arched eyebrows.

Conversation buzzed at Robin's table. "Looks like we've got Gloria Swanson aboard, playing Sunset Boulevard."

"Traveling with her cousin—she says. Calls him Hervy Dear."

Here came Hervy, a big hulking fellow in a sloppy sweater and dungarees, surely twenty years younger and obviously unhappy to be there. Soon as he helped Mrs. Eldridge choose a seat, he sulked over to another table to sit alone.

In their room that night, Robin wanted to swap impressions. "That Hervy—I thought paid escorts were neat looking men who started out as dance teachers."

Steven shrugged. "He has to help her up steps and with luggage. The woman has to be a fool to hire that man, but that's her problem. He looks as if he'd like to silence her with that walking stick. Just stay clear of them."

And he was asleep soon as his blond head settled into the pillow.

Day 4: MUNICH-SALZBURG, AUSTRIA. Free time in Munich for lunch and some independent exploring before mid-afternoon departure to motor through the forested landscape of southern Bavaria to Salzburg.

"Wasn't breakfast wonderful?" Robin asks the Neeleys sitting across the bus aisle this morning. They agree, "absolutely delightful" about the spread of breads, cold meats, cheeses and fruits.

"I brought some along," Robin confides, showing a stash of rolls and cheese in the Globus bag.

"You didn't," Steven groans, seeing her loot.

"It's really a good idea," Joan called over, "the breakfasts are better than some lunches."

Diary: We're on the way to Salzburg. Munich was a 'big stylish city' all right with medieval buildings, lots of trees, no skyscrapers. Hofbrauhaus last night was great. I'm thankful Olga let me have Band-Aids for my heel blisters this morning. I brought the wrong shoes for cobblestones.

Robin doesn't have time to write it down, but something is happening. At the mike, Werner has been telling them about the two German empires that ended after World War I. He just now added stiffly: ". . .that period ended with Hitler and that nonsense. . . . Now! Ve are proceeding south toward Salzburg. . . ."

From midway the bus, a bass voice booms a protest. One of the retiree husbands wants to tell Werner what

Hitler's *nonsense* looked like from bailing out of a B-17 bomber.

Wifely murmurs intervene, preventing a World War II verbal skirmish. Two of the Oregon Sisters start singing, *Lily Marlene* in sweet soprano voices.

Robin nudges Steven. He's silently enmeshed in watching neatly ordered farms and green fields rolling by. Sighing with reverent pride, "My grandfather kept his property just like that when he came over."

Day 4: MUNICH-SALZBURG, AUSTRIA. Sightseeing with a local guide . . . the Olympic Stadium . . . the Oktoberfest area . . . before we motor through the forested landscape of southern Bavaria to Salzburg.

With the heel blisters, Robin stays on the bus while the others climb off to see the stadium, 90-year old Barney with them. She's left with Mrs. Eldridge who leans over the seat to show the jewelry she bought in Munich and tell about what she has at home. Robin nods politely, embarrassed for Mrs. Eldridge being so totally unaware she's a boring braggart. The rings are real enough.

Outside the bus window, Hervy stands there, like a stricken child, grown into the bulk he is now. Looking up at Robin, he's muttering something she can't hear.

Diary: The Hofbrauhaus last night—noisy colorful fun. All that um-pa-pa music going on in all the rooms. Huge beer steins. I took one sip, awful stuff, but you have to order. Steven was cute flirting with the beer maids who didn't pay much attention. I knew he just wanted to show off his German. With all that music, we danced in the aisles like everyone else. Can't remember the last time Steven wanted to dance. Chelsea, the English girl, was talking to some fellow in a leather vest and britches. I imagined all kinds of intrigue. Heard her say of Hervy, "That one's not laddish, but he is a bloke."

Joan Neeley has whispered to Robin: "He was at the hotel desk last night, agitated, wanting to know where the meeting would be. No, we didn't hear what kind of a meeting."

Hearing that, Steven says, "I told you, leave him alone. That fellow is ready to leap on a train track and pull that woman with him."

Day 5: SALZBURG-VIENNA. A pleasant morning stroll with a local expert takes you through the historic center of Mozart's hometown . . . on to a leisurely lunch break on lovely Lake Wolfgang . . . evening arrival in Vienna. . . .

Rain pelts down when they pile out to see Mozart's house, raincoats packed away in the bus. Mrs. Eldridge stays on, but everyone else—the Retiree Couples, the Florida Neeleys, the Oregon Sisters, even Olga with the walking stick, and Barney the 90-year old with his family, climb off and trail down the rainy street, behind the local guide, and upstairs to wander in and out of Mozart's rooms.

In a crowded hall, Robin turns around and there's Hervy in his old sloppy sweater, some kind of angry sadness in his heavy face.

"Died in a ditch, didn't he? Like in the movie?"

Wet brown eyes look down at her, into her, waiting for an answer.

"Yes . . . but he made his music first. And we have it."

Heart thumping, she moves on down the hall, weaving past strangers. For a moment there, she had— what? *Connected* with that awful fellow.

Back on the bus, everyone in place, waiting on two stragglers, Robin searches Steven's lean handsome face. "Connect," she said. "One has to connect."

"What?" Impatient, he watches the bus door. "So inconsiderate, individuals who make the majority wait."

Here came Chelsea, who had been shopping. Finally, Hervy.

Diary: We both got soaked and chilled, but that goes with traveling, I guess—being dressed wrong in the right places. This afternoon, we're heading for the Alps, at last. Steven is telling the New Jersey couple behind us about his great uncle being a baron and how he hopes to meet with a cousin further on. I talked with a retiree wife across the aisle. We agreed Wiener Schnitzel is very dry, but good, like chicken.

"Have you noticed how sweet they are together, Ron and Joan Neeley?" she asks Steven.

"Noticeable because it's usually only sappy teenagers and gays who walk down the street holding hands."

She writes in her diary: *I'm waiting. It'll happen. Something will.*

**Day 6: VIENNA. Reflections of imperial and contemporary Vienna on the guided half-day sight seeing. . . . Start out at the lavish terraced gardens of Belvedere Palace, before driving along sumptuous Ring Boulevard. . . .

In Vienna, it's raining.

Diary: We both have the sniffles. This afternoon we stood in the rain to watch the Anker Clock. These cities are so old and ornate! Steven went walking and saw some buildings that still show wartime damage fifty years later.

Viennese music hall last night was for hordes of tourists, and not as grand as ballroom scenes in a movie. On stage, a pretty couple waltzed to Strauss. Taking aspirin now and going to bed. In Vienna!

At 8:30 a.m. most everyone is in the lobby, with suitcases ready for the bus. Robin had eaten all the fruit she could at breakfast, but the sneezing means she's coming down with a cold.

"Traveling can do that for you," one of the retiree wives offers as Olga shows up, hardly using her walking stick, in a hurry to tell Werner her roommate is sick and has to see a doctor.

Werner frowns, looking at his watch. "Vell, the bus leaves at 9 o'clock."

"Not until the lady sees a doctor." It's the retired bomber pilot who is still irked at Werner. He and two others march off to take Olga's roommate to the hospital while the bus and everyone waits.

Dairy: Guess this cold is making me feel down, even though here I am in Austria, headed for the Swiss Alps. Somewhere in some wonderful place, something has to happen for us.

Having this cold interferes with thinking beyond that, or caring about tromping around the grounds of Schonbrun Palace. Bed is better. Steven stays downstairs, trying to contact the second cousin in Villach.

Day 7: VIENNA-VILLACH. From the urban sophistication of a capital we travel to rustic simplicity through scenic Semmering Pass . . . to overnight in Villach. . . . In the afternoon, board an excursion steamer and cruise on lovely Lake Worth.

Sunshine at last, with a whole afternoon to spend on this terrace with its flowers and the lake sparkling out there and mountains in the distance. It's like being in the postcards she's bought. Steven is off seeing the cousin fifty miles away, had to rent a car, but that's fine since it's one of the things he counted on doing. She hasn't complained once to Steven about being lonely. But then, dammit, not complaining has become built-in habit.

And this kind of scenery should be shared.

The three Oregon Sisters are over there looking at the flowers edging the patio. Joan Neeley from Florida is inside, on the phone, so intent, Ron pacing and waiting.

But there's the English nanny in the black suit and little white collar, sitting alone. "Yes, Luv, sit down," she says sounding so British, and yes, quite willing to talk about Chelsea, telling it with motherly pride.

"I'm her Nana, but I'm like her Mum, and she's good to me as any daughter."

The story sounds like a movie to Robin. This Nana was Chelsea's Nanny since she was a little bit of a thing. Chelsea's parents—important literary people in Britain—were killed in a crash years ago. She's grown up in schools and is always discarding suitors after her money. Now she's tired of collecting degrees and traveling on a whim. Chelsea is going into the tour business. Small special tours, the kind American couples like to take when they're tired of big buses.

Chelsea sweeps up then, looking at Robin, the smile both amused and sympathetic. "And what has Nana told you? I'm a secret agent? No, you told her my new plans? All true. You want a job? Can you get me some groups?"

The thought makes Robin dizzy. For a moment she imagines herself in a neat little office, signing retiree couples up for Chelsea's tours—a much better visualization that the reality of going back to her pay-window job at One Day Auto Repair.

Day 8: VILLACH-ITALIAN DOLOMITES, INNSBRUCK. An unforgettable day in Alpine scenery awaits us . . . the Brenner Pass road to Innsbruck in the Tyrolean Alps . . . to the Italian Border. . . .

The scenery hurts, it's so beautiful—green rolling fields, mountains with snow. Robin can't keep tears from running down her face. Couples in front and on the aisle think she's missing Steven. Isn't lonely and missing the same? She's not sure anymore. She turns on a bright face and lets everybody know he was staying one more day with the German cousin and would catch up with them at St. Moritz.

Today she is almost in the back of the bus, awfully near the gloomy Hervy with his wild curly hair, who stares out the window, away from Mrs. Eldridge's chatter.

Dairy: I've given up waiting on something wonderful to happen. With this cold, can't visualize anything positive.

At the lunch stop, she sits with the Neeleys. Joan's hands reaching for the crusty rolls flash with such beautiful rings, Robin has to comment, saying they must represent a lot of anniversaries, done with candlelight and wine.

Joan lifts both hands and stares at them. "Yes . . . they are . . . from the years." The look she gives Robin is so—what? Sad? "And you're just beginning yours, aren't you? Any children, dear?"

"Not so far," Robin says with a shaky laugh. "Seeing older couples, at least like you two, is encouraging. I guess you have children."

"Sons . . . daughters," Joan says.

"Did you see that Barney this morning?" Ron puts in. "Now there's something to aim for. Traveling the Alps at age ninety. I have to go some to keep up with him."

Day 9: INNSBRUCK, ST. MORITZ, SWITZERLAND. Ascend through the Inn Valley into the Swiss Engadine, a mountain area considered by many as the most beautiful in the world: deep-blue lakes, airy larch forests, mountain peaks, quaint villages.

Head against the window, Robin is angry at her tears and hurting with all this beauty they're rolling through.

These perfect emerald pastures rising to become high wooded slopes, the green so perfect, so clean, right up to the edge of the barns, like a drawing in a child's picture book. A glimpse here and there of two figures, working some simple conveyance, moving about on the green slopes. Where are the cars? Do people walk to these little towns clustered at the foot of the slopes? Do they sit together in some kind of a pub at night to talk?

When she's back home will she remember all this?

The thought sweeps through like an unwelcome reality. Maybe feeding your spirit breaks through some kind of barrier built up where you hide disappointments.

Faces are watching. She manages a teary smile: "I'm fine. It's this cold—and the scenery."

Day 10: ST. MORITZ-LUGANO. Thirteen hairpin bends down into the lovely Bregaglia Valley, then along the sunny shore of the Italian Lake Como, to the southern tip of Switzerland. . . .

Morning in St. Moritz. Where are the rich people? It's Sunday, shops are closed, the place quiet. Their bus group filters out. Looking for a pharmacy, Robin hears gloomy Hervy tracking behind, catching up with her, wearing his second of two big old sweaters, feet plodding along in the big boots.

She has to say something. "Hi—how's your tour going?"

"No better than yours." Glowering, he walks on ahead, down the street, hands in his pockets.

Steven is in the hotel bar, drinking brandy, telling the bartender about his visit with the cousin. No, he doesn't want to go walking in the sun. He has to go upstairs to bed for an hour before dinner. His cold is worse. But he accepts some of her antihistamine pills.

Diary: I'm letting so many sights go by without making notes. Maybe I can fill in later with the post cards. I feel so strange. But I'm still waiting.

Sitting in the sun, Robin doesn't mind when Olga with her walking stick and big old shoes sits down beside her and offers throat mints. Olga reports her roommate, the one who got sick, had to be flown home, back to Oregon.

"You're so brave, traveling the way you do," Robin says. "I came worrying about what to wear. Now look at me, crying over the scenery."

"It's not all bravery, it's a desire to bring sights and experiences back home to one's own fireside. You're young, my dear, but believe me, there comes a time when you grow past certain concerns. And that is not all bad. Young or old, we need to feed the mind and spirit."

This reaches so deep into Robin that the tears come and there's no stopping them. With Olga's arm around her, she collapses against the big bosom for a moment.

Sitting up again, talking into Olga's fleshy, waiting face, Robin pours out some of what she hides inside. The job she hates back home. Being lonely sitting in front of the TV with Steven focused on his laptop. He was so right about everything, so exacting, it made her feel awful not being the same way, feeling his disapproval.

"And what about your approval of his attitude?" Olga asks.

"Oh, he's very . . . Gracious, look at me, babbling away. And here come your friends."

Day 11: LUGANO-ZERMATT. From Lake Lugano to the Italian shore of Lake Maggiore. . . . We leave the resorts behind to board a mountain train climbing the last few miles up to Zermatt, a picturesque cluster of rustic chalets beneath the Matterhorn.

Robin is so thrilled with the mountain train ride up to Zermatt, her head almost clears. Steven looks satisfied too, talking about his visit to the German relatives. It's raining when they get off at the top. Everybody trudges up the steep main street, lined with shops, on past the chalets that seem rooted on the slope at crazy angles, everyone with flower boxes filled with red geraniums. The chalets are as quaint and real as the Tyrolean hats on sale are tacky souvenirs.

Once they get to their room in the chalet further up, Robin wants to crawl into bed. She just might get Steven's attention and let him realize they can be two different people under wool blankets in the Alps.

Diary: Poor Steven, he went to bed really sick with his cold. He drank brandy and pulled up the covers, groaning.

Tomorrow is the special extra excursion, up to the Matterhorn. Not Disney's plaster one, but the actual real peak way up higher behind the clouds.

Day 12: ZERMATT-LAKE GENEVA. For those with a strong heart—ride Europe's highest rack-railway to 10,272 feet for a breathtaking, panoramic view of the Alps from the base of the Matterhorn.

Werner tells everybody at breakfast that not every tour group gets to see the clouds lift and the sun come out on the snowy peak, but there's always the chance they might be lucky. Half the group vote to go, even sprightly old Barney. Steven, after three cups of coffee and his antihistamine pill, decides to go too.

"You'll get chilled and sicker if you do," Robin argues, not hiding how annoyed she feels. No, she's *angry*. And giving up all expectations. She doesn't want to ride on that thing up to the base, even if it is supposed to be the peak experience on this tour.

Down by the shops, on the plaza, she sits on a planter, bundled in her coat, new scarf and knit hat, waiting for Steven and the others to come back down. Waiting now to talk to him, though not sure what she means to say.

Tourists mill around in the cold sharp air, waiting to see if the sun will decide to come out and clear away the clouds that always hide the peak.

Hervy looms up and sits down beside her. She looks straight into his soulful eyes under the wild eyebrows and then away. Okay, if he's going to be a mad-sad killer taking out his problems on her, then okay. She wouldn't feel it, whatever he'd do. At this point, she's not even curious.

"Where's that husband of yours?" Hervy grumbles.

"He took the thing up with the others."

"Wouldn't let old Barney outdo him, huh?"

"Well, I guess. So where's Mrs. Eldridge?" She'd show Hervy she didn't care what he said. Or did.

"She *is* my cousin," he says, with a stricken look.

"Really?"

"Woman has all the money in the family. Sold the farm right out under my daddy's nose. He was a drunk. Let it happen, curse his old hide. I take after him. It's a bitch. I haven't found but one meeting on this whole trip."

"Meeting?"

"AA. What else."

"Well, you're here, seeing the Alps. She didn't drag you."

He looks at his big boots and up again to the cold cloudy sky. "She needed help and was paying my way. I hate the old bitch, braggin' and puttin' on the dog like she was always rich. Started out as poor as my Daddy. Expects everyone to bow down to her now."

"But you came."

"Yeah, I came. Wanted to see something besides Kentucky. Never have been anywheres outa Tennessee and Kentucky."

"Then why don't you enjoy being here?"

"Ha. Look who's talking."

Robin glares into his heavy face, his mouth twitching with a grin.

"That husband of yours—he's a big-feeling stuff-shirt pain-in-the-ass. And you trot along trying to keep up, with him paying you no mind. I know gals at home who put up with such as that. Ones who don't have looks and smarts to do nothing else."

Robin feels hot and shivery all over, searching for something indignant to fling back. She gets up, looking where everyone else is looking, toward the Matterhorn behind its clouds.

Hervy stands too, close enough she can feel his hot breath. "I would of figured you to be too smart a little woman to put up with a jerk."

She walks away, in a hurry, blind with icy tears. At his whistle, she stops, looks back. He's grinning and pointing up. People standing around are all looking up. The sun is shining on the gleaming white peak of the Matterhorn.

She waits, taking in the silvery white summit. A special thing happening. Or the beginning of it.

By afternoon, in the chalet, Steven is in bed with a fever. Robin comes in, sits in a chair, watching. He looks miserable, blowing his nose, wadding up yet another tissue into a neat ball and stuffing it in a bag.

"I want to talk," she says, "about the expectations, the hopes I had for this trip."

"I don't," he mumbles.

Poor thing. He's sick all right. "Just the same, Steven, I do."

He sits up, glaring between coughs. "You want to talk now?" His voice is a rasp. "If you insist, Robin. I meant to tell you later . . . at home." More nose blowing. "I intend to make some changes. First, in the office."

Robin is sure the changes are not anything she had in mind. "Office? What does that have to do. . . ?"

"I'm adding Ruth as a partner." He grabs another tissue.

Is he actually blushing or is that all fever? Now she gets the picture. Ruth, that stick of a young woman, that haughty brunette he took in how long ago? Rude anytime she had stopped by the office. "So how do you two control freaks get along?" Robin asks, knowing everything all at once.

"I don't want to talk about it now," he rasps.

She walks over, picks up his sack of balled tissues and rains them on his blond head. "I do. So talk."

Day 13 and 14: LUCERNE. Welcome to two lovely days to stroll about Lucerne, visit the famous covered wooden bridge, and see the ornate patrician houses lining cobbled streets. For first-hand look at alpine merrymaking, attend a folklore party with yodeling an alpenhorn blowing.

Walking around Lucern by herself, watching white swans in the water by the bridge, Robin goes over all of it again, as if she's some detached person, remembering a scene in which she and Steven were the players.

Steven rasping and blowing and saying they wouldn't have come on this trip if it hadn't been paid for.... And how for some time he's been planning to say this ... and she's forcing him to say it now ... but this marriage isn't working. And yes, he and Ruth.... Well, he wouldn't go into that.... But once they got back, he would be moving out and he didn't intend to discuss it any more right now.

Day 15: Your home bound flight leaves today. Travel with Globus again!

In the hotel lobby, waiting for the bus to take them to the Frankfort terminal, crazy adrenaline pumping like an excitement she's not ready to dissect yet, Robin goes around hugging everybody good-bye. These are special people now because they've shared an important experience in her life whether they know it or not.

She goes looking for the Florida couple, the Neeleys. Finds Joan at the phone booth in another serious conversation, crying. Joan comes out, not hiding the tears, to say, yes, she'd love to hear from Robin again. Goes into her leather purse for a card. It says Joan and Mark Krone, Sarasota, not Joan Neeley of Fort Lauderdale.

"My dear," Joan says quietly, nodding to the phone, "I was checking on my husband. In Sarasota. He's Alzheimer—for four years now. Doesn't know me but I still check on him, even when Ron and I take a trip. You're young but you must know—life delivers its curves. Curves lead to new hopes—if you allow. Ron and I have known each other for years. His wife died three years ago."

Robin hugs her back and goes looking for Chelsea. Finds Nana instead. Was Chelsea really going to open a travel office in the U.S.? Could Robin write to her? She would like to talk about that job.

She catches Olga coming out of the elevator. Hugs her. Olga says, "You come see me in Eugene anytime you want to see Oregon."

As the flight lifts off, Robin looks over at Steven, who is really sick, poor thing, eyes clinched shut. If she stayed quiet and careful of his mood, he'd be apologizing before New York. Just to save routine if nothing else. *Ha. No way.*

"Hey, Steven, wake up. Listen." Ignoring his guilty glare, "You were right about me being the dreamer. It was a self-protecting device I had to use, living with an unbending perfectionist. Notice I said *was*. No, listen. I knew something special had to happen on this trip. You have to admit I was right. I just didn't know what it was going to be. Now that it's happened, I want you to know how much better I feel."

Steven blinks, opens his mouth, closes it.

Poor thing, she thinks, he looks miserable as well as surprised. A control freak who's lost control. What a pair he and Ruth will make. She wouldn't want to watch.

"No, don't say a word. You go to sleep. You can, just put your mind to it. I'm going to visit around the plane before the movie."

At the upward thrust of the jet, her own head opens up. She can breathe. Good thing she's strapped in. She feels so . . . unattached . . . floating in new space.

Marian Coe

Another Spring for Tulips

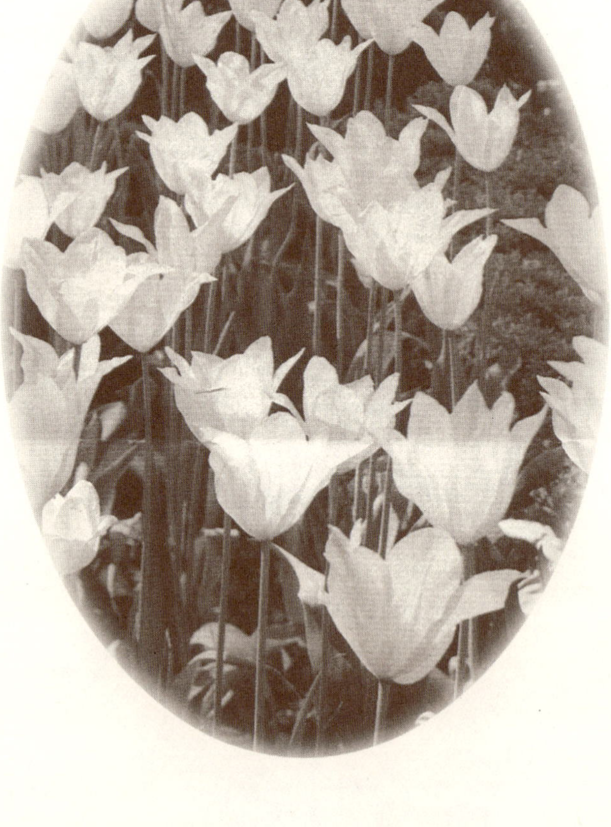

Another Spring for Tulips

By noon, the visiting nurse is there. On the sun porch, Emily tucks the blanket around her husband's shoulders, presses his limp hand, and goes out to meet her lover.

The path winds through what was once a garden yet tulips and jonquils have come up as if this were any spring. Beyond the apple trees, the gazebo waits, its fancy white trim lighted by the weak March sun.

It is here she sits, sweater pulled tight, eyes closed, waiting. Determined choice shuts out the sound of the traffic on the road below, once quiet and green-bordered as a country lane. Now cars race by, heedless of what they pass and leave behind.

Sometimes she thinks he won't come. She chides herself for needing this visit. It takes patience to wait but she has learned well about patience these months.

When her stillness is complete, she is aware of his approach. Behind her eyes, she sees his lanky amble, the shape of his tousled red hair, the clipped beard shaping a strong face. She glances once more through the apple trees, down to the house, before acknowledging he is there in the gazebo, with her, a vital man she has loved from the beginning.

"I'm glad you're here," she says, not yet wanting to face him. As always, he asks, tell me how you are.

The answer comes like a whisper. I'm here. The jonquils and tulips are blooming. The days pass. Another morning comes.

When he answers: I wish with all my heart I could make it easier for you, she says: You do, by coming to me like this.

She dares see him now. The clipped beard, grayed a bit. The eyes alert, warm. Did he wear the old tweed jacket to amuse her?

Smiling, she thinks of the first time they talked, walking across campus, her freshman fall, when this tall fellow in a sweater fell in step, already the admirer. Discovering he was the young lit professor the other girls swooned about over their Frank Sinatra records, she'd said, arch and sassy, "I thought real professors wore tweed jackets and smoked pipes."

Remembering that now, she laughs. The sound comes out like a sigh. The gazebo is silent again, yet alive with memories.

I loved you from that moment, he always says.

Still happy, she asks: Remember the Algonquin?

She was in New York for some sorority thing. When he called to take her out she wasn't supposed to let the others know. How quaint that caution seems now, the need to hide new love. Yet, isn't the memory more delicious now?

I tried to walk to the Algonquin and got lost and had to call you there, she murmurs. You came, brought me back. We sat at a table against the wall, you telling about the Roundtable, Dorothy Parker and friends, as if you'd been there yourself. I even remember the heavy silver coffee pot on the table as I drank in the moment.

He is quiet as the breeze around them, but as always, he finally answers, You were so young. Did I ever tell you I saw the woman you'd be? Strong.

You told me many times. It helped make me strong.

And stubborn, he says with a soft laugh. You didn't want to leave your new job. So you told me to go to take the position at Stanford without you.

Forty years ago, the faint breeze seems to say.

Forty years ago, she repeats. So many seasons of busy living separate that time and now. She is silent again, looking out and down at the gnarled apple trees and the old, struggling garden. Both are putting out shoots of a new spring. Perhaps buried memories are like roots, giving meaning.

Again he asks, How are you doing? Tell me how it is for you?

She can feel the urgency, knows it means caring; that it has never ceased even through these long years between then and now.

I'll tell you how it is, she says. I remember reading a child's story about a boy lost in a snowstorm. He found a fence, and held on, moving post-by-post to keep from giving up and blowing away. That's how it is for me now. The fence is routine. I make it post-to-post.

It helps, this speaking of her thoughts. They come out in a whisper of fact, not a complaint. She adds in a stronger voice, the days have become routine, a routine I've accepted, embraced like those posts.

If I could only make it easier for you, he always says. She feels the grip of his strong hand.

I know. And knowing helps.

Below, the traffic roars up again. It can be blocked out just so long. It's all right, she says. I can let you go.

She stands, breathing in the morning, nourished inside, resilient, with a new flush of strength.

Walking back, Emily stops to pick two red tulips and four yellow jonquils. From inside the sun porch, two figures wait. She goes in, hands the blooms to the visiting nurse, this stout capable woman who has become one of the posts she leans on each day.

"We're doing fine," the woman says, nodding to the man in the chair. "Let me put these in a vase."

Emily takes one red tulip back. Sitting close to her husband, she holds it up to his vacant gaze. When he focuses, she puts the flower in his open limp hand.

Waiting—she has learned to wait—she strokes his arm, his tousled gray head. Watches him study the perfect red petals.

Speaking softly, clearly, into his lined face, "Remember when we planted the perennials out there? Same year as the apple trees? Before the back road became a highway?"

He looks toward the garden.

"Remember," she says, "I loved tulips so you had tulips in your place when I first came to Palo Alto? And you met me wearing a new tweed jacket and a pipe you never smoked?"

"Stanford," he murmurs.

"Yes! And remember way back, that first time in New York when I got lost looking for the Algonquin and you came and found me?"

He turns his head to study her, a searching look struggling behind his face. "Emily? . . . Are you lost?"

"Sometimes I am," she says, her fingers closing over his. "But not always." She feels the answering tension in his big hand, sees his slow nod, and knows everything this man—once lover before the busy married years—would want to say if he could speak the words.

Marian Coe

Gifts to Be Delivered

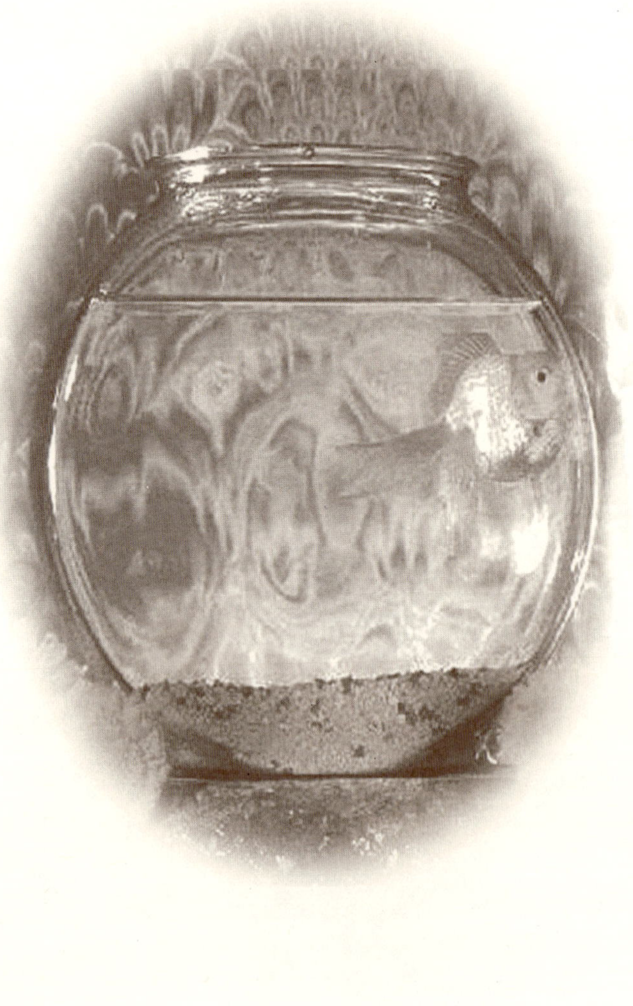

Gifts to Be Delivered

My neighbor Harriet is a gusty, no-nonsense little woman, I give her that. When she says I'm a soft-hearted trusting fool dealing with the public, I usually nod and smile and go on doing things my way. Until this week. For three days now, I'm wondering if she's right. It's an awful feeling.

Harriet manages the Tropic Isle next door, twenty rooms, pool, and shuffleboard court. My Gulfbreeze has fifteen, no pool, but shade from old sea grape trees. Both places are the mama-papa kind on the old part of this gulf front, but we're close to the water, which is more than you can say for the new high rise resorts.

"Lily Gray," Harriet has been preaching to me now for a year, "you aren't careful enough who you check in. Your Alabama grandmother might have run her boarding house like a big-hearted mama, but it's a different world now. You read the papers, don't you?"

She keeps reminding me weirdos don't have to look like rock musicians any more. "What looks like a regular fellow can murder a girlfriend in your motel bed. They get a TV movie made about them, but *your* business goes down the tube."

Harriet means well and she is smart. Ran her own cleaning establishment in New Jersey before she lost it to a philandering husband and came down here to Florida. You should see her chasing stray boys out of the Tropic Isle pool. Of course those kids sneak right back that night, just to pester her. I'd try something else myself.

This morning I take my coffee and book up to the second balcony as usual. By 10 o'clock most folks have gone out to the beach for their dose of Florida sun, or gone off for a day at Disney World. The cleaning lady is downstairs and will call me if anybody needs me. It's my hour of peace and quiet, unless Harriet comes over.

I sit here, not opening my book, wondering about that Maryland couple in 5B. I'm waiting up here to see if they're going to come out to the beach today with the child, and acting normal—I hope. I checked them in three nights ago, a young couple in their thirties with the boy about five. The child whimpered and stayed scrunched up in the arms of his daddy, well, I take for granted this is the daddy. The thin blond wife looked preoccupied. They both went out without asking about restaurants and the like, the way people usually do, even when they are road weary like those two. Foster is the name, in a rented car. Seems like anytime I pass 5B, the blinds are drawn. Makes me worry.

In the past, I would have knocked on the door and asked what I could do. For years I treated my guests like family, that's why I had repeats. Nowadays I squelch the notion because people are so touchy about their privacy.

Maybe Harriet is right about not trusting folks. Or I'm getting as suspicious as she is. The idea takes the shine out of the day.

I set my book aside and squint out past the top of the seagrape leaves. Under the sun, the gulf glitters all the way to the horizon where it turns dark blue. Today it's rolling in with a lazy rhythm. Everything looks normal out there. That bright white curve of beach is dotted with browning bodies. You can smell the coconut lotion all the way up here in a good breeze. Along the foaming edge, bikini girls are strolling and toddlers digging.

There goes the Maryland couple, trailing down my little board walk toward the beach. Now why aren't they dressed for the hot sun? She's wearing shorts at least. They're holding on to that little fellow's hands, practically dragging him along.

Wouldn't you know, here comes Harriet, her flip-flops slapping up the back stairs. She plops down in the other deck chair, stretches out her brown legs and pulls a pack of Marlboros out of her waistband. In the red halter and white shorts she wears, and those big sunglasses, Harriet looks for the world like a scrawny old bug-eyed bird, though I'd never hurt her feelings and say so.

Harriet lights up and heaves a sigh with her smoke. "What you reading today, romance or that positive thinking crap? Lily, sixty years shoulda wised you up."

I ignore that.

"Is the Hertz Chevy couple still here with the frightened-looking kid?"

"They're staying three more days."

"Something fishy about that pair. That's why I told them I was booked."

"They're out there now."

Harriet cranes her neck to squint at the beach. "Yeah. Look at that, will you? He's dressed like a bank clerk. At least she's in shorts. I saw them in the tee-shirt shop last night, buying them. You shoulda been there."

We watch. Foster has picked up the boy, walking toward the surf where other children are running and splashing. Not this boy. He's clinging to the man's arms. Now they're heading back. Oh, my. I ask Harriet what happened last night.

"The kid was hiding under the racks crying, the clerk complaining. They picked him up and got out of there fast."

I listen, more grieved than I let on. "Something's real sad there," I admit.

"Sad, smad." She waved her cigarette. "They're hiding something. The kid, most likely. Probably kidnaped him from some court hearing. Or worse. The things that can happen curl your hair. You ought to watch the talk shows instead of the stuff you read."

I shift my chair out of the line of her smoke, but the look she gave me burrowed right in. Some awful imagination rose up about the Fosters from Maryland.

"Harriet, I can't call the beach police and say the people in 5B look unhappy and stay too long in that dark, air-conditioned little room and have to drag their baby to the beach."

"See, you know something's wrong."

"I've thought of going to the door with some oatmeal cookies. I made them last night thinking that. I've thought of asking them to let the boy come look at my tropical fish tank. Play with that kitten I rescued. Have cookies"

"Cookies. Geez. You might have a couple of kidnappers or molesters in your place and you're thinking of giving the boy cookies. Look. They're coming back in now. Carrying that kid." She stands up to watch. "You better do something or some newspaper story will say those two were here, in your place and you didn't kick them out."

"I can't kick out people because they look troubled, Harriet."

"Give them some excuse. Say the plumber's coming."

"That won't help the boy."

She shrugs her skinny brown shoulders. "Tell the police to stop them on Gulf Boulevard for a check. Main thing, you won't be involved."

Soon as Harriet leaves, I go downstairs, feeling miserable, and walk past their room. The blinds are drawn. Back in my room behind the office I sit like a worried lump, squelching the urge to go comfort that little boy.

I don't need Harriet to remind me you don't invite a strange child into your place these days to eat cookies or watch tropical fish. I could do this sneaky thing, take this plate of cookies and go to the door and ask how he is. They're so closed-face they would say thanks and shut the door.

The front bells rings and I have to go check out a sunburned family and sign in a new group who want to know about deep sea fishing. Then here comes the cleaning lady to get paid and I have to listen to her troubles.

When the office is quiet again, I go back and look at the plate of cookies, ready to be delivered. I'm standing there debating. Now the bell rings again. It's Foster at my front desk, looking as grim as ever. I can see his wife is sitting in the car holding the boy.

"We're moving on," he announces.

I don't feel relieved one iota. I blurt out, "Is your boy all right? I've been worried about him." I look right into that young man's face and he eyes me straight back.

"In time . . . he'll be all right . . . I hope." He puts down his key and walks out.

"Wait!" I follow, waving my arms and stop him by his car. "Mr. Foster—I must talk to you."

"Yes?"

I say what I had wanted to say for three days, knowing it's not what Harriet would recommend. "*Is there anything I can do?*"

He looks hard at me, his mouth tight, face the color of his hair, pale ash blond. I see now how young he is, but like someone grown old in a hurry.

"I wish," he says, the words flat and final. He looks away, toward the sunset colored beach, but I figure he's seeing something dark in his mind.

I wait. He must feel me waiting because he turns back and says in this cold voice, "Tad is my brother's child. Or was. Something pretty bad happened to my brother and his wife. And Tad saw."

It's so quiet for a second, only the breeze in the sea grapes moving.

I must have made a little sound because he goes on, biting it out. "After it happened, his grandmother was keeping him. Then she died." He opens his empty hands, shrugs.

I give a helpless "Oh."

"We have been advised Tad needs a psychiatrist, maybe extended professional care. My wife and I haven't dealt with children—or anything like this—but before we gave in, we decided to try giving him this trip. We had hoped . . ."

He stopped again, looking out at the gulf. "Bad things can happen, you know, Mrs. Gray."

"I know they do." Never have I denied that. I have to ask, "What did you hope for?"

"Something good to happen for him. He's frightened of any stranger now. We wanted him to see other children playing on the beach. We hoped people would smile and talk to him. Hoped he'd see the world isn't all bad."

"If you had told me—"

"You don't ask people, hey, be kind to us, this kid you're frowning at is not just a crying brat. This boy is a traumatized child needing help, to know he can trust again."

He grips the keys in his hand. "So—the trip was a lousy idea. Didn't help. We're taking him back to the doctors."

Even as I say it, I realize I sound like a foolish old woman, foolish only because it's too late. "I wanted to invite him down here to . . . to see my tropical fish. I kept thinking. . . ."

His smile is cold. "That would have been nice. He misses his grandmother, besides the other thing. Thanks anyway."

I watch him turn back to the car, drop himself in, and start backing out. I hear myself shouting, "Wait! I had cookies. . . ." But he's wheeling out to the boulevard and into the moving traffic.

Back in my room, I sit in growing shadows, heavy with remorse. In the lighted tank, my tropical fish put on a show with no one to watch but a kitten. The phone rings. It's Harriet screaming to high heaven that the boys had put seaweed in her pool. I tell her the Fosters are gone and why.

"Ahah! Told you."

"But they were the *victims*."

"Well, you never know, do you?" Harriet says.

"That's just it, Harriet—*you never know*."

I don't try to explain. I don't say, it might seem safe to stay back in your own space and distrust everybody. But that way you miss the ones who need trusting awfully bad at that moment, and you've left them out there and you end up making the world less safe for everybody.

I hang up. Go out to the desk. Check in a couple, a big bossy fellow, and a nervous girl who might be eighteen, but maybe not. He wants to know the closest liquor store and he's off.

I watch the girl standing out front, arms folded, biting her lip, as if she's not ready to go in. Or maybe she's looking at the last streak of sunset. I'm going to call her in here to give her the cookies. Don't care if she laughs at such a silly thing. Just maybe she needs a friend and a telephone. Who knows for sure unless you offer?

I've decided. Harriet has her way and I have mine.

The Healer

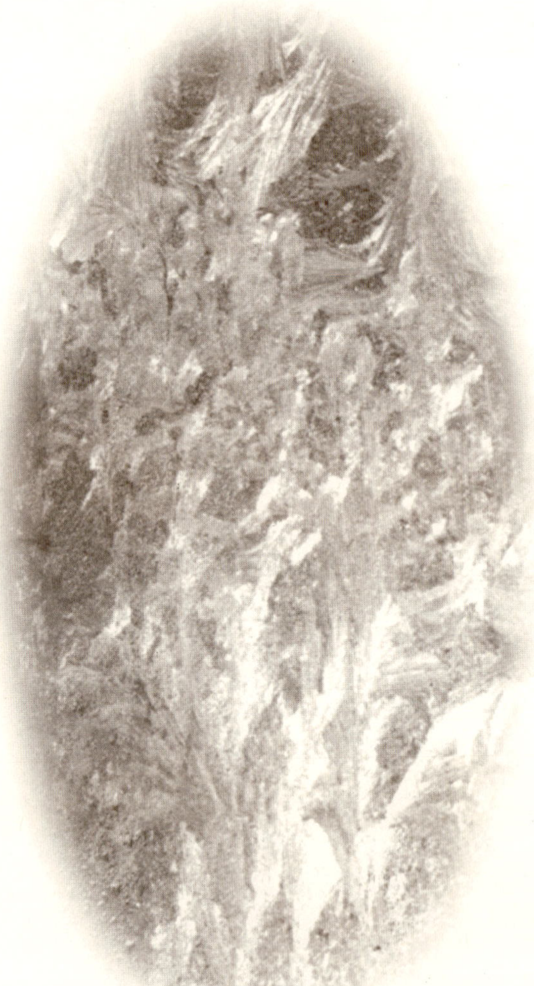

The Healer

Friends tell me, oblique apology in their voices, "They say he's a healer, why don't you . . . ?"

"Go see?" I answer, pretending to smile. "You really think he can raise this body from the dead?"

I don't say: he's just a man; he can't change what happened. Yet this cold morning I close the door on silent rooms and walk toward this so-called healer's house. I see myself as from a distance—a woman moving stiffly down winter streets, shawl-wrapped, like the wounded thing she is.

If this man dares preach love, I won't be tricked. I'll say: *Why do you think I'm here?* Love is vulnerability. When it's taken away, what was once a flame becomes an aching void. The pain of emptiness becomes flash frozen. I know—my chest is an ice cathedral.

Is this visit a fool's trip? Yet I keep walking, too numb to care, or turn back another way, the paper with the healer's address crushed in my cold fist.

I pass a playground where bundled children stomp and run, voices like bells in the chilled air. One child stands close to the fence watching this woman trudge past then turns away. Did she see my eyes? Did I make her sad about growing up? Shamed, I want to call her back, but no sound comes.

It's just a house, this healer's place. A woman opens the door, nods me in. I am shown the basket for the money I should give. She leads me down a hall. Says: *Lie down, relax*, and goes, closing the door behind her.

In this silent room, a narrow bed waits, sheet drawn smooth and white as a marble bier. Gray light from the frost covered window makes no shadows.

He comes in, stands near, angular face and veiled eyes above me, looking down, studying this body, this silent disbeliever. Long fingers touch and close my eyes. Perhaps he sees I have really died. The fingers trail my forehead, their touch like hot ice.

When he speaks, the words are quick and terse. "There is an energy flow that comes to us from the universe, connecting with the life within the body. You are blocking it out, by holding what you hold inside."

He goes, leaving me to my cold altar, knowing anger.

Did I come here to prove no man can be a healer? Or secretly wishing for a miracle I vowed to reject?

You say I'm blocking out the interflow, energy of life, by holding on to what I hide inside?

Holding, sir? I would say *contained* inside. I know too well the reasons I am wounded. I could spend hours giving proof but I've spared listeners all the rational reasons I am hurt. Yes, and how angry I am at being dealt this fate.

Yes, righteous rage, contained and nobly frozen from public view. Where is the relief in acknowledging this? Where's the pride in letting go?

The room is silent as a waiting breath. Shadows move on the ceiling. I sit up, legs dangling, limp, to watch the frost-bound window turn crystal from a sudden thrust of winter sun.

It's pale sunlight, yet the frozen glass begins to cry proud ice. Streaks of it allow color to slip into this chilled and silent room, touching my clinched fists. I let them open.

Melting window ice reveals a glimpse of morning out there.

Watching, I let it happen. Let go of the frozen torment, felt as ice daggers in my chest. The breaking free is a different hurt, a flare, pushing up through a tight throat, coming out as hot silent tears. Victim tears? No, freeing tears. I push them out until the holding chest is empty and quiet. Yet—alive.

Outside, the healer waits, an ordinary man, who lounges silent with his coffee. At the door, my hand is warm, his hot, as we shake and nod and turn away. There's no need to share each other's secrets.

Back on the winter sidewalks, I walk fast, face up to tingling air. At a young tree, I gather branches for a bouquet to take home, in memory of something once in my life but no more. As I walk, one stem bobbing against my lips, I taste the hard kernel of a bud.

At the playground, children turn to watch this woman walking with her arm load of leafless branches. A small girl comes to the fence, asking questions with her eyes.

"Look," I say, showing her a stem with its column of buds. "This means spring is coming. A whole new summer is waiting in this bud."

When friends ask, *What was he like, the healer?* I say, He's only a man. When they persist, *But your voice, you sound more alive*—what can I say?

How to explain about melting windows? And the moment of choice?

Pretty Is As Pretty Does

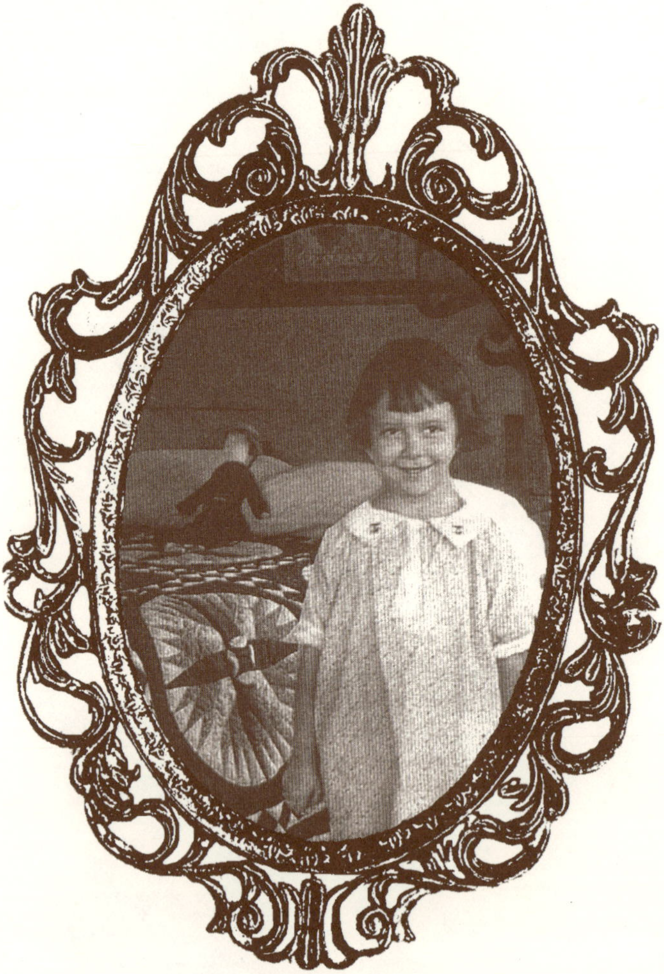

Pretty Is As Pretty Does

*T*hirty minutes *after the plane clears* the gray wool skies of Los Angeles, Ali is wondering what in the name of heaven possessed her to do this crazy thing. If nothing else, she could have used the four-day weekend at Palm Springs practicing the relaxation response.

The over-spiced Bloody Mary doesn't help. Nor the book she's brought along to study, *Dealing with Parents of the Disturbed Child*. At her elbow, the fat fellow on the aisle, punching his laptop, keeps breathing noisy as a runner. Ali leans against the window gazing into limbo space. Well, that exactly matches her feelings.

Below, ridges of brown mountains spread out in eerie silence, reminding Ali how much distance she has kept between herself and Alabama. Until last week when Jaime hadn't called, and she had this four-day weekend waiting, saved to spend with her only, too-busy daughter.

She'd looked through the *LA Sunday Times* travel pages for something totally different to do—a private change, a breather, a weekend lark. Nothing triggered the least bit of interest. In the bedroom, away from the noise of Duff's golf game on TV, Ali got out the address book and looked at various numbers where Jaime might be reached. No, she wouldn't call again and leave another reminder.

Digging deeper into the bedside drawer, she brought out an old address book, a saved thing. Inside, a two-year-old Christmas card with a telephone number and a short scrawled message: "Hi, Alice Ann. I'm back at the old homestead, would you believe? Here looking after Daddy, in his old geezer stage. Kate."

Ali dialed the number. Fidgeting, she listened to it ring. A woman answered with husky nonchalance. It was cousin Kate, all right. Ali found herself rocking on the bed, grinning into the phone, saying, "Baby Kate, guess who?"

"As I live and breathe, it must be Dotty Brown. Where are you? Still out there in LaLa California?"

Ali imagined her own laugh trilling across the country. Oh, how perfectly ridiculous, how funny, those old kid names coming up like that, as if they waited, like graffiti embedded on the brain.

"In LA, sure. And you?"

Kate drawled back, "Gawd, yeah, the old place out at Huffman. You aughta see it here now. Yeah, your Uncle Harry is still among the living. Wouldn't you know that rascal would outlive them all? He'll be glad to hear I talked to Alice Ann."

With a sudden surge of pleasure, Ali found herself saying, "I just might fly out next weekend and look at the old hometown."

"Then I'll meet you at the airport, and bring Bitsy Blue along. Once we get talking, we'll have Nonnie spinning in her grave."

Promising, Ali hung up, made the flight reservations, called back to give Kate the arrival time, and hung up before she could let herself back out of the whole idea.

In the TV den, where Duff stretched in the recliner watching the action on the greens at Pebble Beach, she announced, "I've done it, found something different to do this coming weekend."

She started picking up scattered Sunday papers, talking to the top of Duff's balding head, not minding she was probably talking to herself.

"Did that daughter of yours finally call?" he asked without glancing up. "Look at that drive."

"Kate—my cousin Kate—says we'll have Nonnie turning over in her grave."

Duff frowned. "Who?"

"Nonnie. My mother's mother. I've told you. Webster's dictionary could run her picture next to 'matriarch,' Southern ever-loving bossy variety. She's the one who stuck us with the silly names. I might have been Alice Ann back there, but to Nonnie I was Dotty Brown. The first time she saw me—at six pounds—I had big brown eyes, like dots. Or so she said."

Ali sat like a dreamer, holding her armful of papers, saying out loud what she was seeing, for her own amusement.

"Cousin Betty was a preemie, 'big enough to rest in your two hands, blue eyes looking at you,' Nonnie told us a million times. So Betty was forever after Bitsy Blue. Kate came last, so she stayed Baby Kate in the family until she went off to Auburn. Once she was so mad being called that she pushed a fist into Nonnie's mashed potatoes."

"Yeah?" Duff sank deeper into his chair, watching action at Pebble Beach.

Ali went silent but kept smiling. Some things get lost in translation, and one of them was explaining southern family habits to someone who grew up in New Jersey.

One hour out of Birmingham, Ali stands in the humming cubicle behind the Occupied door, touching up her eye shadow, pumping her champagne hair and worrying. The vibrating floor drops, then heaves up again, her stomach doing the same. She gives the mirror a testing smile and tells her reflection: Okay, you're space traveling into the past.

And why? Really, why is she doing this? It's been twenty-seven years since she'd bailed out of the home town, out of sight of family expectations, and except for Christmas holidays from college, then later, quick trips to necessary funerals, she'd never been back. Her own mother had died before taking over the matriarch role. Nonnie had posed for her ninetieth birthday, the picture sent by some cousin. Maybe Bitsy.

Will they even recognize one another? Lord, that's a worry. She hasn't been brunette Alice Ann for eons. Her chin line is better than it was five years ago but they couldn't know that. Kate and Bitsy will probably get the idea people do go blond and stay younger in California and she's flying out for the weekend to flaunt the proof.

Bragging is not good, Ali remembers. The bragging one will be tolerated coolly, replied to briefly with arched, silent reproof and the transgression will be gossiped about later.

Back in her seat, Ali decides, when they ask about her life, she will tell them, brightly and casually, about finally getting her Master's and the new responsibility at the agency. But no, she won't elaborate. She won't be *uppity* about it for heaven's sakes. She might explain it's a funded private agency where she gets to deal with pregnant and runaway teens pissed off at their rich parents. Should she say Duff owns an insurance firm, or not?

Definitely, she'll tell them how successful Jaime is. Certainly she has a right to report her only daughter, at twenty-six, is PR director for a chain of hotels up and down the coast. The pleasure of mentioning that at any opportunity makes up, in a way, for how little she sees of Jaime.

Under the plane's belly, Birmingham is there, spread out in its valley. Rigid in her seat in its upright position, Ali looks down on a mixed map of past and present. From the tilting jet, there's Red Mountain and Shades Mountain still looking green . . . freeways slicing over downtown streets and there's the rusting steel furnace that used to pour out firey red ore as the city bus rolled past on the Viaduct road. Do tourists actually go through there now?

In the terminal, gripping her carry-on, she scans the crowd. A clutch of ruddy-faced young men mill around, cheering some departing hero whose massive young chest fills out a University of Alabama tee-shirt. This calls for swallowing back emotion, seeing how some things never change. Crimson Tide fervor for one. She sees that also, some things do finally change, of necessity. The hero is ebony black.

Walking toward her is a lanky woman in a long denim shirt dress and sandals. It's the causal, don't-give-a-damn look Ali would expect in Santa Fe or San Francisco. But this is Kate herself. When did the brown hair become rust red, tied into a pony tail?

It comes back in a flash. Kate has lived a few places besides the old home town. A card came once from a commune in New Mexico. Bobbling after Kate—a short chubby woman, encased in polyester print. *Deja vu.* The gray-permed head, the shape—it could Bitsy's mother, Aunt Gussie in the flesh. Only Gussie has been dead for fifteen years, at least. It's Bitsy Blue herself, who hasn't been Bitsy for a long time.

Watching their approach, Ali stops, rooted, aware of her size 11 California designer suit and her champagne hair. Did she actually come to prove something? To see verified in their faces—what? How well she's doing now, in spite of all that's gone on in her life these past twenty years? That would be too *tacky.* Oh no, another Southernism cropping out.

The three converge. Shoulders are hugged. A moist Bitsy clings a second, planting a kiss on the cheek, before stepping back, smiling like Aunt Gussie, the blue eyes not so blue but brimming behind her glasses. "Dotty Brown, it's really you." The rising inflection hangs there at the end of the sentence like a vague question.

Kate waits, arms folded, grinning. "Gawd! It really is. Right out of California with the ill winds, heathens and

Oscar nights. Let's go. Nonnie is watching from on high and expecting some good old family palavering. Daddy is rocking on the porch, can't wait to see Alice Ann."

Silently, she follows this blithe, forty-four-year-old cousin and Bitsy out of the terminal. Should she remind them she hasn't been Dotty Brown since a child and not even Alice Ann since the first marriage? That memory pops up now like a once-read Harlequin romance with a lousy ending.

Kate leads them to an ancient green Buick that shows its wax marks. "Daddy's car. He gets out and shines this old hearse as if he's expecting to drive it through the Pearly Gates."

Bitsy has huffed along, talking grandbabies and how time passes. She needs to sit in the front so she won't get carsick. "You don't mind, do you, Alice?" Ali crawls into the back against hot plush upholstery, pushing aside a pile of magazines about antiques.

"My junk," Kate says. "Dump them on the floor." She maneuvers the gate and sweeps out to the road.

"Yours? I remember you hated Aunt Millie's English bone china and the rest. Called it her fussy old stuff."

Kate wags her head. "Yeah. Remember when this was a small airport? Bitsy, hold the grandbaby pictures. Alice needs to see where she is."

Ali leans back, not sure she does, but here she is in this hot back seat, behind the brassy red and mousey gray heads of these people she knew as children, Kate drawling, Bitsy chattering. When are they going to ask about her flight and her life like proper hostesses, collecting the visitor? They're beyond the airport now, traveling ordinary here-and-now roads that seem to be superimposed over the ghosts of remembered ones.

Turning, the Buick is rolling now down narrow, familiar side streets, slowing past frame houses and front porches that look back like old faces of forgotten neighbors. This is still the old East Lake neighborhood, for sure. Her ball-bearing roller skates knew these sidewalks, the rough spots and the smooth places.

"Oh, we needed to do this together!" Bitsy cries, her voice a shaky trill. "How long has it been since we were together? Not since Nonnie's funeral. I remember having two little kids at home and being six months with Jimmy when I looked into that casket. Alice, you came from somewhere with your little girl and wouldn't talk about being divorced. She had black bangs, your little girl." Bitsy gives Kate a reproving glance, for all the world looking just like her own mother thirty years ago. "It was Baby Kate here who didn't come to the funeral."

Kate shrugs, hands on the steering wheel, letting the car ease along. "I was still in my GI wife period off in Frankfurt, thankfully. Not that I liked Germany or that particular husband. I mortally hate funerals. Nonnie would have reared up in her satin lining and promoted a chorus of 'Be Ye Kind'."

"Oh, no!" Ali realizes she has just squealed. "That Sunday School ditty. *Be ye kind, be ye kind. . . .*"

Bitsy sings in a wistful soprano, "*. . .one to another, be ye kind.*"

"And what about the one line lecture: '*Pretty is as pretty does*'?" Ali says. Good lord, when has she thought of that phrase?

"Save me the reminder," Kate says.

"Now, Kate." Bitsy goes back to figuring out dates. "You were at Aunt Millie's and Uncle Harry's the spring I had Jimmy."

"Then I was on my way to Albuquerque. After Germany. And about to enter my soul-mate period," Kate says. "Can't quite remember the fellow now, except for his hot chili. But I liked Santa Fe. Had a little shop before everybody else discovered the place and the rent went high as the San Andros mountains. Take a look, Alice."

The Buick is idling past a small building, a dead thing overgrown with vines with a faded For Sale sign.

"The drug store," Ali sighs. Inside that once important place, she sipped a fountain Coke, her fifteen-year-old self thrilled by the James Dean lidded appraisal of a curly-headed blond boy. Lord, what an innocent, family-protected body she'd been, a child from a different planet compared to the diffident teens she deals with now.

"You don't want to look inside the old high school," Kate says.

"No, I didn't want to. Why? Is it gone?"

"It's still here," Bitsy says. "My two girls went there. Those halls, that auditorium where we sang 'Hail dear old Woodland High, noble and strong' to March Slav? You wouldn't believe it now."

"Taken over, you'd think, by creatures from the Rock Star lagoon," Kate says. "Remember how our lockers were such sacred trusts? Now they look bashed in. No, not by guns, just adolescent anger and instant gratification. How you doing back there, Alice?"

"Okay." She's riding through a forgotten reality that makes the apartment back in LA, and Duff himself, fade to a mirage.

"Imagine telling a kid today, 'pretty is as pretty does'," Kate says. "Every one of them, all our aunts included—provincial, innocent, stubborn, determined to make us in the same mold Nonnie expected of them."

"Can't imagine," Ali says. But thinks: translated, maybe it has a certain pragmatic logic?

Bitsy sounds wistful. "I miss those big old family gatherings. I was seventeen when I married Billy. Remember, just before you went off to college, Alice? I thought I was getting away too. I was back in two years with two babies and a third coming. I never got away. You've got to see my grandkids. They're a handful."

The Buick wheels into a wide asphalt drive, stops in front of a low brick building. A grinning Kate turns back to Ali. "Well? Do your Dotty Brown eyes see where you are?"

Ali recognizes the big oak tree to one side, the lone shade for this hot white cement. That tree used to be in the back yard with peach trees. Daddy's strawberries grew where the cars are lined up now. The Buick, idling now, sits about where the living room was.

Because both their faces are turned, waiting for her response, Ali says, "Disorienting. My room was right about over there." She swallows hard.

They drive out, with Bitsy talking and sighing. "When you've been here all along, you don't see things changing, though you know they do. You don't have time to think about it when you have a husband who doesn't want to be one. Then a second husband who died right at the kitchen table. But I shouldn't complain—except for Jimmy being in the army, marrying a Japanese girl I've never seen. I have a nice apartment near a good supermarket where my second daughter works."

Ali is dealing with too many old images long packed away. Her mother, for one, standing in the kitchen of that house, wiped away from the earth. Her voice comes out small as a sigh. "I'm glad your house is still there. Glad Uncle Harry is still alive."

Kate snorts soft derision. "He's too pig-headed to die. And don't expect the house to look like it did when Mother was around. Gawd, that woman was Miss Neatness Herself. Got it from Nonnie or else it was passive resistance reflex from being married to Daddy. Did I ever tell you the old guy had a girlfriend back there for awhile? Until Mother drew him back in line. We kids weren't supposed to know.

"I remember," Ali says, "your mother's phrase about 'A place for everything and everything in its place'?"

"Yeah. This kid declared freedom from those orders at age five only no one got the message."

Bitsy says, "No matter how you screamed. I never dared do that. And you, Dotty Brown, you'd be behind a couch reading." She turns around to tell Ali, "Uncle Harry is just fine. Thanks to Kate, he is. When Aunt Millie died, I was just so afraid he'd fade away."

"Stubborn old cuss," Kate says. "Remember when Nonnie ruled the roost and the whole family kowtowed? You remember who didn't? My old man. Lord, how Daddy roared about having to pack up and family-gather at Nonnie's?"

"Sunday afternoons" Ali murmurs. "And Thanksgiving and Christmas." Did she ever tell Jaime any of that? About family gatherings on holidays, and the summer picnics, too. The aunts would be setting out fried chicken and chocolate cake, the cousins playing under the oaks. A flash picture comes of herself in a swing, holding on to the ropes, pumping herself high, feet pointing to the July blue sky—then firm hands at her back. Nonnie's hands, steadying the wobbly swing.

"I wanna do it myself, Nonnie."

"You are, Dotty Brown, but you're going whomp-pejawed and I don't want you to bang yourself into the bars."

"My son Rick," Kate is saying, "my one and only offspring, is Air Force in Germany. That's where he started. Funny, isn't? Maybe you pick up vibes or something where you are conceived. Oh, enough of our boring kids. It's Dotty Brown's time. What's life like in California, cousin? What's it like without a stubborn old man to nurse and a barn of a house to keep up?"

Duff seems so far away at the moment, Ali can't see his face, or where he fits into her life, the feeling part that's a lone private place, the part that's always wondering when her daughter might remember to call.

Ali says finally, "I remarried ten years ago. He's in insurance. My daughter Jaime, the little girl you remember with the black bangs? She's likes her work and makes a lot of money. She's too independent and busy to get married." Leaning back against the hot plush seat, Ali thinks: So busy I can wait three months for a phone call.

"My girls got married about as quick as I did," Bitsy is saying with a sigh. "Wish they hadn't, to be honest."

Kate picks up speed past new apartments and McDonalds and Wendys and an old time Bar-B-Que. "When Mother and Daddy built out here, it seemed the end of nowhere, place for boy cousins to play cowboy and Indian. Damn, but I was jealous. It's all grown up now. Real *Southern Living* homes all around us. When you have any acreage at all, they bug you to sell out."

From the busy highway, the Buick turns up a private road. Once woods were here. Now a grassy expanse and gravel driveway leads up to the two-storied white frame house Ali remembers. As the car chugs up, she imagines people on that wide porch, the smell of fresh pole beans cooked with pork, and Aunt Millie's lemon cream pie waiting on the sideboard.

Someone does get up from a porch rocker. Uncle Harry himself. Ali senses the coat and tie are in her honor. She goes up the worn steps toward him, seeing how time has siphoned the brawn and the juice, leaving a shell of a pale old man who is happy at the sight of her.

Flapping his arms, ready for hugging, he rasps out his welcome. "Look at her, will ya? Alice Ann, all the way from Callyforn-eye-A. Wouldn't live there on a bet."

He stands there beaming, something of the old devilish glint showing behind the glasses. "One thing I wanna know."

Ali waits, breathing in this place, the past and present flashing together. "Yes, Uncle Harry, what do you want to know?"

"How 'bout that old Buick? She still looks good, huh? Buicks outlast those old Studebakers your Daddy brags about. You had a good ride here, right?" He sinks back into his rocker, looking proud.

Kate leads the way into the wide hall. "Don't mind him. Lives in the past. Now, Dotty Brown, put your bag in the front bedroom while I rustle up some food. If there's laundry on the bed, dump it in a chair. I warn you, I don't keep house like Mother. How 'bout iced tea? Or bourbon. We don't have to hide the stuff now. Time marches on, helping here and there, screwing up the rest."

Kate heads for the kitchen. In the wide hall that smells of old wood and polish, Bitsy waits, hands clasped over her belly, eyes brimming. "Now you look around, you hear? I'll go help. But Kate has it all ready."

Aunt Millie's front guest bedroom still seems a place of honor: the crocheted spread and sheer curtains dainty as the woman was, the heavy bureau as solid as her beliefs. Beyond the open window to the porch, Uncle Harry rocks alone. Below the steep lawn, traffic sends up a faint hum.

Ali puts her overnight bag down in a needlepoint rocker. In the bathroom mirror, she looks for her California self but sees only the room behind her, the old fancy lavatory with its brass fixtures, the silent room scented with lavender. How can one feel so disoriented by familiar sights?

She wanders back into the hall, and on into the big living room. It's a silent stage, waiting for actors who won't come. The dark face of a huge TV is the only incongruent interloper. Nothing else seems changed in spite of Kate's protests. On the old grand piano, top covered with tapestry, gardenias swim in a crystal bowl, sending out the sweet smell of funerals or high school graduation.

A cluster of framed photos pose there, groups taken at family gatherings, the still young or middle aged. Smiling out of one is the soft face of her own mother who died at fifty. And her father, standing dutifully with the other sons-in-law, aunts and uncles behind Nonnie. Sitting at her feet, a young Bitsy and a skinny Kate and her own seven-year-old self.

The voices from the kitchen now might be the voices of her mother and aunts chattering with sassy confidence, as if their houses, their family, their streets, and the town spreading beyond them were their own God-ordained center of the world.

"Y'all come," Kate calls out. "Hope your appetite wasn't spoiled by airline play food."

In the dining room, the table is ready, gardenias in the center, four places set with Aunt Millie's kitchen china, the old Blue Willow. The good stuff shines from behind glass cabinet doors. Even the heavy silver pieces look polished.

In this high-ceilinged room, organdy curtains barely moving with warm summer breeze, Ali has to rub her chilled arms. This is too much. Why did she come?

Bursting through the swinging kitchen door, Bitsy and Kate set filled dishes on the table. A platter of sliced ham with candied yams, bowl of green beans, basket of corn muffins, sliced red tomatoes. Next comes a tray of glasses, iced tea topped with mint and lemon.

"The chocolate cake is good as Aunt Milly's," Bitsy promises.

Kate shrugs. "Hell, we hafta eat. Now to get Beautiful Dreamer in."

By cake time, Uncle Harry is teary with pleasure of an audience for his tales. "Don't encourage him," Kate says.

"Daddy, I swear I'm going to put you on stage and charge admission."

A car honks out front. Bitsy pushes up from the table. It's one of her sons-in-law here to pick her up. She gives Ali a moist kiss on the cheek, catches a teary breath, hears the horn again and struggles out. Kate says, "Poor Bitsy. Tell you about it in the kitchen. Do you remember how to dry dishes? My dishwasher is out."

In the beginning night, Ali wanders out to the porch rockers, to wait on Kate. Below the drive, traffic is beginning to make a moving chain of car lights. She rocks slowly, behind porch vines, looking at the wide lawn where once a garden and trees once made a fine place for hide and seek. Once upon a time yards like those represented limits, and within those limits, security, but playing there supplied a certain adrenaline magic, because playing out there on a moonlit night, you somehow imagined how it'd be when you grew up and would be free to go beyond those boundaries.

Moonlight through the vines patterns the porch by the time the front screen door whines open, and Kate drops into the next chair.

Back in the kitchen, Kate had spun stories with glib irony. Now her voice is quiet and rueful. "Sorry it took so long. Takes time some nights seeing that the old man takes his pills and gets himself in bed."

They rock in unison, feet propped on the banister. The yellow cat settles on the railing, sniffing the summer night. Kate murmurs. "Glad you came, Dotty Brown, even for a quickie visit."

"Me too." And why had she? For some reason. . . .

"Poor Bitsy Blue. She's had a rotten life. Has heart trouble, did she tell you? And not on Medicare yet. Right now she'd rather be here but had to go baby-sit those grandkids. Her children make use of her. That girl never did learn to say no like some of us did. Gawd, we yakked away and didn't give you a chance to talk about California."

Ali keeps on rocking.

"You're working, big deal job, huh?" Kate says.

"It's the burn-out kind. I deal with pregnant teenagers who never knew anyone like Nonnie." She means it as a flip remark but it doesn't come out that way.

"Look at that traffic down there." Kate murmurs. "Go on."

"Your son in Germany, does he ever call? Does he let you know what kind of adult he turned out to be?"

"Not really. I don't push. Someday I'll fly over there, walk in and say, guess what, here's your Mama. I won't stay long."

Ali rocks, listening to crickets, dealing with what waits inside but never gets said. "For most of Jaime's growing-up years it was just the two of us. I taught my daughter it was okay, being independent."

"Our reflex, cousin, from growing up in this family of hugging, loving females overseeing your life. My mother. Yours, the whole clan of aunts."

"Well . . . she missed that." She stops rocking, needing to say, hear herself say it, "Jaime plans these big party weekends for travel writers, at five hotels along the coast. I keep waiting for an invitation. She keeps promising to invite me sometimes, then just . . . seems to forget. I'm thinking—maybe she doesn't know it's really important to me." Ali intends to leave the confession there but the rest of it comes out as she thinks it. "I've given her so much space, it stays, like a void between us." The silent question rises and leaves a chill. *Does Jaime know I love her?*

"They don't want anyone running their lives, Alice. I didn't either back there. I've got the same piss and vinegar in me as Nonnie. And my old man. Only I have to use it my way."

Ali rocks harder. "But you knew they cared."

They are silent a moment until Ali says, "Remember how your mother used to talk about a happy medium? I think she had something there. Is that what we've missed? The girls I counsel, they've had freedom as kids, but I doubt they ever felt strong hands at their backs." She can hear Nonnie's voice saying "don't want you to go whom- pe-jawed."

"Different world now, Dotty Brown."

The yellow cat struggles out of Kate's lap and back onto the banister. "Damn you, Scutter, can't you see I want to love you?"

"Be ye Kind, be ye Kind," Ali prompts.

"Weren't they something back there?" Kate muses. "Poor Bitsy. She never got away. We did."

"But you came back, Kate."

"So have you, Dotty Brown." Kate's shadowed face is smiling.

"But you seem to be staying, Baby Kate."

"Well, hell. There's Daddy. And this barn of a house full of Mother's things. Actually, they're valuable now. By the way, do you want to take something home? Before I catalogue it all and go into the antique business here, fancy price and all? My stuff is dumped upstairs. I'll move up there in time and deal downstairs."

Ali pulls in a deep breath. Below, headlights stream by. "You'll put a sign down by the road? What will you call it? For Sale—Mama's Fussy Old Things?"

"Mmm, I've thought of Nevermore Treasures. You'd better choose something while you're here."

Ali stops rocking and sits up. *So that's why I came here.*

"Matter of fact . . . yes, I'd like to take something back. Maybe that's what I came for. Not any of the china. What I want is one of the pictures from the piano. One of those with all of us smiling bravely into the camera."

It would be her gift to Jaime. She'd say, "Look, Miss Independent Achiever, maybe I haven't told you, but you came from family."

Marian Coe

The Sentencing

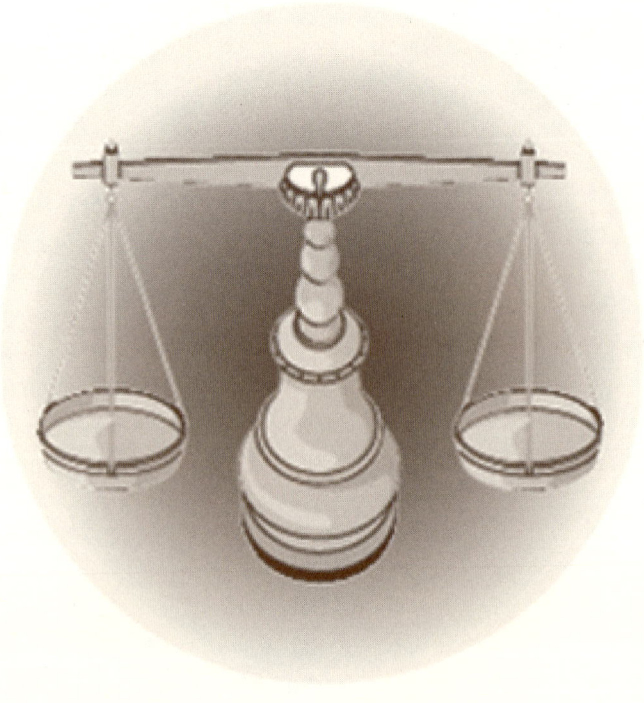

The Sentencing

August 5: Today, for the final time, I reenter the courthouse. As I pass, curious spectators move aside. They know who I am. The press has identified me as the father of the victim who sits stoic-faced and silent each day of this trial, staring toward the son-in-law accused of the crime. Their stories should have said, ". . .the father who must watch as yet one more powerless spectator."

Today, I refuse to be powerless. I arrive with a plan.

The courtroom's conditioned air is never a relief. Now, waiting for the judge to return to the bench, the air is electric with rustling tension and whispering debate. We wait for the jury's decision, knowing the man will go free, saved by the law that allows no reasonable doubt, yet denies admission of my feelings, which are facts.

I have listened to his lawyer mocking those who almost saw what happened. Have watched the accused as he proclaimed, with an actor's false remorse, that the tragedy began as a lover's quarrel; that my daughter was not pushed, but fell from his car into oncoming speeding traffic.

I know my son-in-law. He knows that I know. On the stand, he avoided my steady gaze until he had to meet my eyes, causing his words to stumble for a moment before turning away to continue the smooth stream of lies.

That is when my wish became a knowledge, a plan.

In my sixty years, I have never been a vindictive man. But how does one know what one is capable of, given the reason? Neither do I sanction violence. It was this young man's violence, hidden from others under his cunning public exterior, that cost my daughter pain, then death.

No, my plan is different. It is revenge, yes, but justifiable.

The judge is on his bench now, demanding quiet. The jury files in, blank-faced. Next to me, a woman leans close to whisper, "You must feel so helpless."

I have been, but not now. The judge warns there can be no outcries or strange movements in the courtroom. My plan requires no overt action. This is personal, intensely so, and must be done quietly, from my soul to his, who murdered my daughter.

I watch the back of his head as he waits up there with his lawyer. His movements are jerky but with a certain nervous exuberance as the jury takes its place. The verdict is read in flat tones of duty. The "Not Guilty" is no surprise, yet I sit like a stone. The courtroom's tension breaks into guttural murmurs. Voices drone. People stand. It's over.

Impatient, but focused, I move with the flow, out to the crowded corridors to deliver my own sentencing. I pray I will have that chance before he can walk out to resume his arrogant life. Can one pray for help to deliver vengeance? Isn't it righteous revenge?

The hall is a hubbub of reaction, people blocked from the acquitted by his lawyer.

I move toward the two of them, making my own path, my face set, my manner calm. At the lawyer's frown, I call out that a reporter wants to picture us together. But I am the one who moves in, close to the murderer's chest and gloating stance. He is startled, then angry, to find my body—no, my breath and stare—so close to his own.

Chin up, he mutters, "You heard the verdict, old man. Get out of my space."

I murmur, "It doesn't matter" with such cold calm I trap his surprised attention. With deadly assurance, I deliver my sentencing; send it into his widened eyes, quick as a twist of a knife.

"It doesn't matter," I repeat, "because the heart inside your chest will begin to tighten, your liver will atrophy, and your testicles will begin to burn."

Startled, he gasps, tries to smirk, but can't twist away from my face before I seize another millisecond to say into his, calmly, as one would intone a fact: "It's beginning now—can't you feel it?"

His eyes flash with uncertainty. He draws back against his lawyer, who grabs for my arm, but I have done the thing. I turn away, into the crowd, leave the noisy corridor for the hot, empty street outside.

August 30—I lie awake these nights, unsure if my plan has worked, still unfreed from the smoldering, helpless rage. From my rumpled bed, I renew my sentencing. I visualize the murderer's pumping heart, the vital liver, imagine both tightening, turning gray and sluggish. I fall into fitful sleep telling him his groin will burn with no relief.

September 10—Today I have learned news of my son-in-law, the freed murderer. His sports car sits for a week in his driveway. He is ill. I hear this with a strange feeling. Is it surprise? No, humbled wonder at the potent power of a wish. Have I found the answer to retribution, safely hidden and personal? It breaks no law.

October 6—An autumn of confusion. No longer do I take long walks to ease my tensions or clear my mind.

Finally, today, I sit in front of my friend, my doctor, who says, "Glad to see you. By the way, that son-in-law of yours ... did you know he's here in the hospital again? In intensive care. The bypass didn't work and now his liver isn't functioning. No cancer, but unusual pain. Thought you should know. Now, about you—?"

I shake my head, ask only for a refill of my prescription, potent capsules for which I have begun to take in excess, seeking temporary relief. Why submit to x-rays and probing, for answers to this tightening of my chest, the gut that has become a secret enemy, and the burn in my groin?

On this gray day, in spite of the pain, I leave his office and walk. I sit now on a park bench, alone by the bay, confronting the results of my plan.

How tragically normal, how justifiable, is the need to relieve the dark anger.

How unoriginal the desire to wish retribution on the person who caused your loss.

And how inevitable to discover revenge yields no freedom, the need only keeps the pain alive.

I sit like a stone on the bench, knowing this, watching the bay's hidden currents wash flotsam against the seawall, leaving the open waters glistening under changing light. A man is more resistant, more stubbornly proud of his right to pain than his need to forget.

At the seawall's edge, I look down at the rhythmic flow that leaves debris and moves out clean. Clutching the bottle of drugs in my hand, I stand here wondering which need I dare drop into the moving waters.

Marian Coe

Visit to a New Improved Jungle

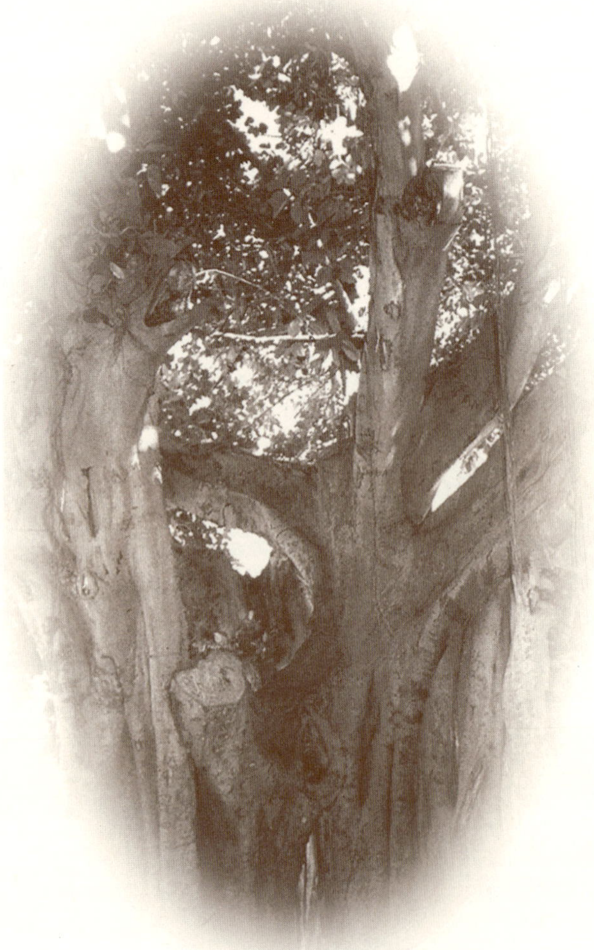

Visit to a New Improved Jungle

Uncle Homer, *just be patient. I deliver on my promises. I'll get you home.*

We should be getting close, but I can't be sure. We've got this rain to deal with, and ahead is nothing but red tail-lights of a crawl-and-stop traffic. Sky is gray as a wet mule.

Here's another lit-up billboard promising the Good Life in Tropic Towers. Must mean these buildings, sticking up like upended egg-crates with twenty floors of little windows. Here's one just started. Looks like a concrete Tinkertoy.

Uncle Homer, we've been away too long. You're not the only one needing to get back to your old house in your own patch of jungle. Been a long time, but I'm eager to see it again, too.

Lord, how all of us kid cousins loved that place, those tangled vines, the lagoon with Smiley, the alligator, the old house hidden back there like something out of a Hansel and Gretel story. No witch and gingerbread, but we had a rascally old bachelor uncle who let us camp out at night to watch raccoons. I even came back from a husband in Tennessee to visit you, before they hauled you out of your rocker and carted you away—for your own good, they said, because you couldn't see well enough to take care of yourself.

Windows are steaming up in here. Have to open them to breathe in Florida again, different from East Tennessee hills. Only it smells like wet pavement and traffic. Cripes. Where's that nice salty wind from the bay? Has to be close. They've put up steel Tinkertoys, but they can't move the bay, right?

Did I take the wrong turn off the new interstate? We passed the same veteran's hospital back there, same palm trees and lawns, just shrunk back for the wider road.

I think we're getting close, but Lord, I don't see your jungle ahead. Uncle Homer, be prepared. These yellow wheeled robots churning away in the ditches. They may have gotten as far down as your place. Another robot just ahead is bogged down, sick from gorging on sand and roots. I have to tell you—they might be able to wipe out a place natural as your jungle.

But they couldn't do that to the banyans, could they? Who would kill those huge ancient things? The boy cousins wouldn't let me climb with them but you set them straight. I climbed as high as any of them, right? And I was a better dreamer, once up there. I sat up there, like a real tomboy, but listening to birds, like a secret princess. The boys tried to spoil it by whooping like Tarzan.

We're crawling now, can't help it. Maybe we haven't gotten there yet. Maybe your jungle is still there. Oh, what a special place for a kid. All those exotic plants you brought in from South America way back when. You'd tell us how the banyans started eons ago in India, before some were brought to Florida.

This messy rainy stretch we're on—could this be the old sandy two-lane road that went past your place and old man Colley's grapefruit grove? This car-chocked four lanes, plastered with these billboards touting Tropic Towers?

A traffic control guy is standing up there in the rain with a flashlight. I'll just roll down my window and ask:

"Oh you, sir, out there. . . ."

"Hey lady, what's the problem? This traffic is slow enough."

"I'm looking for banyans."

"Right lane, next exit, keep moving and watch that bulldozer off the road just ahead." Muttering, "Damn idea having an opening night when the road's not finished."

Uncle Homer—is that a fantasy my windshield wiper is smearing for me? My mind playing tricks? Up ahead, where your woods always hovered like a great dark green shape—that's the exit he means. We're turning in now and I see a banyan, the one closest to the road, with a lighted sign at the base, like a showtime marquee.

I'm reading: "Banyan House Restaurant . . . Parking . . . enter here."

Got to roll with the tide, and the tide is this right lane traffic turning in past the bulldozers.

Lord, Uncle Homer, you won't believe it. Your jungle is mostly cleared off like some giant thumb came down and squashed it, leaving only your three biggest banyans, floodlighted at the base like ancient creatures, captured and hung with lights.

And your old house? It's turned into something like a picture I saw once, I think it was called the Taj Mahal. It's lit up like heaven itself.

I'm being waved into a big parking place, way to one side. If this is just right of where your jungle used to be, then it has to be old man Colley's place, his orange grove. Where his dinky fruit stood facing the sandy road.

That old hermit has to be turning in his grave, knowing fifteen hundred cars are lined up tonight on what was his grove, the whole earth sealed over with shiny black asphalt. Don't answer, Uncle Homer. It was enough, having you remind me of my promise to get you back here.

Car doors are slamming up and down the line, people piling out, squealing in the misty rain, skittle-skaddling between the cars, heading for that fancy lit-up building. We have to follow. Boys with flashlights are saying, "Step right this way ladies and gentlemen, excuse the construction, paths are just now going in. . . ."

Here we go. Listen to those grumbles as we track along. I'm thinking this is the same soft sweet Florida rain that peppered the lagoon when we cousins watched for Smiley to come up. Sometimes there was noisy rain, roaring through the trees, flapping leaves, rattling palm fronds, birds squawking, real jungle sounds. Rain could stop, just like that, leaving the moss dripping from that big crooked oak by the pond in front of the house. Then the moon could come out, making ghost shadows on the pond.

I remember you leaning against that oak, flipping pipe ashes into the silver black water. I always suspected you went out there to talk to the moon, since you got impatient with the opinions of most people, including those who brought us for visits. I used to see you out there and think the moon shining on your pond probably answered.

Well, you weren't an overly friendly fellow, you know. Remember that string of Heritage Club ladies who minced down the path from the road, wanting to take pictures of the banyans? And what about the fellow who looked like Ichabob Crane with the bushy brows who sat up on the road with his avocado sign? You marched up there to make sure old Icky wasn't doing commercial business on your property. Then Colley let him move over to his side, just to get one over on you. I know you three old guys argued about everything under the Florida sun. I always figured you had a good time doing it. Wouldn't be surprised if you still do.

Well! . . . Here we are in front of this lit-up monstrosity. I know, I know, we came to see a sweet old boarded-up house, the pond in front, the lagoon in back. But you always said, one has to do what one has to do, so I'm keeping my promise and doing. Only thing now, have to figure out how.

I hope you know I am the only one of the cousins who would do this for you.

An intercom is saying, "Party 243, party 245 to the Sultan's Room."

Lord help us, here's a marble entrance where the old porch used to be, with tourists strolling around ogling and ahhing.

You'll be patient won't you if I figure this out with the help of a Martini? I know, I'm strictly bourbon and water, but standing here, like a displaced person clutching this tote bag as if it's my last possession, well, I need inspiration.

Down this hall of gift shops, here's a cozy looking entrance called the Raja's Lounge. Inside, all dark red lights and draped with oriental tapestries, weird music seeping out.

Even listening to Siam music, why do I get the feeling this must have been the kitchen? I'm thinking turnip greens cooking in salt pork on the stove right where a young guy with a Sultan's hat is putting out a tall glass of something yellow. I might as well try one of those. A girl in a harem skirt with eyes like a raccoon brings it over.

Uncle Homer, I almost lost you in there. I was wandering around, kind of dizzy on that yellow fizz drink, and picking up vibes. But the belly dancer girl followed, asking me, "Is this bag yours?" Nice of her, but then I had left a fifty cent tip. If she only knew where she was, her black-lined eyes would widen and that sassy mouth would drop open.

Out front again now, wondering how to go about this. No, the question is *where*.

Thank the Lord, I see the answer. On the other side of this sweeping front drive, there's your old oak, Uncle Homer, standing there in this strange night, hanging with moss, by the old pond.

They've made a little path with a wrought iron fence around the pond, so nobody will fall in after one of those yellow fizz drinks.

Ready? The rain has stopped and the moon is trying to shine on the water. Opening the tote bag, I take in a deep breath, and slowly, let it out again, as I let you out, Uncle Homer.

No, wait. This calls for some words. Let's see. To the pond and the moon, I say: "I commit to you, this ornery, uncommon fellow, the uncle who taught me to love what grows natural and what should be protected. He wanted to come home. Good-bye Uncle Homer. You're here."

Marian Coe

Voices and Places

Woman in Front of the Tube, 1998

Office days behind her,
she yields now to unwanted labels,
>accepting senior discounts to shop on Tuesdays,
>spending mornings, tractable, in front of the tube
>enduring Kathy Lee's effusions
>or Days of Our Lives, which is not her life,

waiting for Rather or Jennings or Brokow
to report tonight

on new speculations
from the nation's Capital,
revelations couched with alleged,
supplying fodder through the evening,
for talking heads to repeat ad infinitum,
swapping lines, straight-faced,
about libido and lies
like comics on Saturday Night Live,
while replaying film clips of the women
who have decided

Marian Coe

    their lives have been stained
    and harassment sustained
by some past private moments with a man in power,

Watching,
the woman in front of the tube,
remembers the bald-headed boss
whose offer made her face burn,
and the co-worker in the cab with his hand up her leg
and the friend's drunk husband who
    pushed her down on the master bed
    as his wife downstairs called for more ice—
moments she fled from
    and quickly packed away
as the unwanted things that loom in life,
    happenings best forgotten,
    not dwelled on,
    like a car crash avoided or worse
    the stolen purse, her heart chain inside.

The woman in front of the evening news
remembering how she walked away
pretending she was still untouched,
choosing to forget unwanted moments,
sits here now, surprised by guilt,
wondering
if the women swapping privacy
for book deals and talk shows and loot
are wise or fools . . . and
which was she?

At Home In Front of the Tube, 1999

My Sony set is for entertainment,
as well as scenes from the current wars
political and otherwise,
so I have a right to escape —don't I?—
from what challenges my comfort?
For sanity's sake,
I turn away from the repeated sight
    of school children running for safety
    court scenes of blank-faced adolescents
    and adults' dismay,
    empty of answers.
Changing the channel
when you can't change the world
calls for quick finesse,
a ready finger on the remote control
as stricken faces zoom in,
real ones from yesterday's news,
or a culture idol crashing cars,
weilding guns in glory colors,
death defiers thanks to special effects.

Tonight, choosing to be amused in front of the tube,
I click past movie mayhem and dead-eyed gunman
to stop, instead

at this pretty room, empty, no, curtains move,
a figure crouches,
silent stalker, knife blade gleaming—
>   always the knife is gleaming,
>   always the female is preening
>   before her mirror, cornered now
>   screaming.

The rescue is too late, always too late.
Her slitted white neck spills red.
>   —always too much red

Why care?
My carpet's still clean,
as commercials cavort pushing pizza and pills.

Now Jay Lino swaggers about my living room
talking to himself.
I turn him off. Sit in silence.
seeing endless flickering sets tonight,
tending and training a child
in the thrill of crashing cruisers
and love as sex and sex as assault,
unlimited lessons on cutting throats,
and vengeful satisfaction of
firing into brains.

I sit in silence,
wondering—
on some evening yet to come
will that crime-primed child
grown man-sized, but soul-robbed,
be the intruder at the door of what I thought
was this safe living room?

Brochure Lures

"This is no ordinary place. . ."
invitations murmur over glossy views
of undulating mountains
". . .older than the Andes, more ancient than
the Alps, carved by the ages. . ."

". . .rolling into blue distance
with introspective majesty. . ."

"high sanctuaries still. . .
domain of the Parkway. . .
where the Appalachians rise to their highest crest and
merge with the sky. . ."

"Come fall in love. . .
Come home to the mountains, closer to heaven. . ."

"...*discover your own private retreat...*"
with security gate, premier golf course...
the perfect escape for a week, a month, a lifetime..."

Postscript from an *Appalachian Journal*
on the marketing of the Blue Ridge:
"The appeal is ancient,
but clothed in the language
for our time.
Serenity, luxury, exclusivity...
'Life as it should be lived'...
Remoteness no longer a disadvantage,
but an asset. The word *escape* is key."

Excerpt from *Eve's Mountain, A Novel of Passion and Mystery in the Blue Ridge*

Eve's Mountain

Mountain High Magazine

May 1986

Off The Beaten Track column

Here's one for stressed-out souls wanting to step out of the twentieth century for a breath of serenity: a true hideaway hamlet — if a resident ghost hovering around doesn't spook you. (Her name is Eve.)

We found High Haven in the Blue Ridge Mountains of North Carolina, a curious old summer colony perched on its own secluded ridge, an hour's drive north of Asheville, adding 45 minutes of switch-back drive up to Crest Road.

Before highways brought change into the Appalachians, hamlets like this, with its summer hotel, were a presence in these southern highlands. No more. For curious reasons (some say the ghost), High Haven remains a place-out-of-time, an Appalachian Brigadoon. No marquees and motels on this ridge.

The venerable Ridgeway Inn sits against slopes (yes, called Eve's Mountain) like a proud old lady ignoring the outside world. "Amenities" here are the antique beds upstairs, rocking chairs on the verandah, and a music box chiming you in to dinner. From a rocker you get an open view of rolling, smoky blue ranges stretching to infinity, the air bracing as a breeze off a mountain stream even on an August evening.

There is a catch.

Off The Beaten Track...

Most of the rooms stay filled by innkeeper Edmund P. Dilworth II's season regulars. Still game for the getaway? You'll find cabins for rent, hidden around on these wooded slopes.

Along Crest Road you'll also find: A "Country Sundries" with a marble soda fountain, hot soup served. "Previously Read" where a dedicated book browser could stay happily lost within narrow aisles of loaded shelves. Next door, crammed with an amazing collection, true to its name, is "Maggie Hardy's Old Timey Things."

Mornings, the small U. S. Post Office (hung with stuffed bears) draws summer people from around. They pick up the mail and their *Wall Street Journals,* swap news of the heat in Florida, and congratulate one another for being "up here, not down there."

Shop owner Maggie Hardy may invite you in, put on the tea kettle, get down some of her china cups and point you to a high-backed rocker. But don't ask about the reported ghost. Curiously enough, we found the Eve mystery a touchy subject among Havenites when we checked out the hamlet this past summer. However, the story gets retold at mountain folk fairs. Story tellers of old mountain lore add the Eve mystery to prove "strange things can still happen in these ancient southern highlands"— once you get away from the highways and fairways and reconstituted Main Streets.

Okay, the story goes like this:

On an August night, some forty years ago, before good roads cut into the Blue Ridge, Eve Kingston—a city girl who loved the mountains—

Off The Beaten Track...

put her infant son to bed upstairs at the inn, walked out into the night (tearful, old reports say) and disappeared. No trace, no clues ever found. The following year, the successful young husband returned, bought up most of the ridge, promising disgruntled mountain natives he would not develop, nor strip the old growth timber, but would keep the mountain in its natural state, "in loving memory of his lost Eve."

The romantic version about this Appalachian Brigadoon goes like this: Eve's ghost is protecting the place from change. The other version calls it an unsolved murder and asks if ghost sightings on the back side of Eve's Mountain mean she's hovering around, (time being no object?), "waiting to do vengeance on whoever did her in."

Maggie Hardy shakes her head and tells you firmly, "High Haven is the last unspoiled place in these mountains because everybody *wants* it to stay that way." Everybody means year-rounders like herself, summer regulars, and mountain families in the hollow below Eve's Mountain.

What about the major landowner? Alexander Kingston, husband of the lost Eve, a wealthy fellow who cleared off the top of the mountain for his big summer place, Capstone, with helicopter landing strip.

"We don't mind. Mister Kingston has kept his promise not to sell off any of this ridge. That means no bulldozers and billboards can come in here to ruin the peace and beauty."

So, is High Haven closed to all but its season regulars?

Off The Beaten Track. . .

> "Lordy, no. We get curious tourists rolling through here, spring through fall. Some who rent a cabin are lover-couples, you can tell. Then there's always a few new faces who show up alone, trouble behind their eyes. I figure they need to be here. Hideaways, I call them. We just have to hope they don't spoil what they come for, you know, and that's a kind of sanctuary."
>
> *Your Off the Beaten Tracker*

April, 1986
At **Perloin Productions'** Atlanta bureau

From his cold spring week on the Appalachian Trail, Russ Bern showed up for the Monday morning news desk meeting, still on an adrenaline high. *Perloin's* new tabloid show needed mysteries to uncover and murders to expose. Russ walked in pitching a story he had found and checked out.

To six assembled crew members, glum-faced over their coffee mugs, Russ promised, "Here's one the coast will okay. It's got everything—great visuals in a mountain hideaway you wouldn't believe, where a so-called romantic ghost tale has been serving as cover-up for the major landholder who murdered his wife."

Yes, a hot name was involved—Alexander Zackary Kingston Sr., CEO of Kingston Industries. "We can blow him out of the water with no libel problems if we go in this summer, shoot their ghost reports—which shoots down the legend. We leave the guy to his fate. A cliff-hanger show. . ."

Excerpt from the novel, *Legacy*, a seductive tale of suspence, mystery and family secrets played out on a 1945 Florida Gulf Coast, on the eve of postwar change.

Florida Gulf Coast
Grouper Hole
Restaurant & Bar
May 5, 1945

By eight o'clock, the brassy wail of Harry James' trumpet poured from the juke box and through the smoky haze of Grouper Hole. Middle aged tourists filled the tables. GIs and local girls leaned close in the booths. At the bar, the old fellow called Cap'n, mixed it up with garrulous younger men, the burr-headed GIs out on their weekend pass.

Chuck's warning about the weekend action hadn't changed Lelia's calm insistance. "I want the job." On this, her first Saturday night, she glided quickly past their "hot damns" and reaching hands.

Hazel waited at the scarred upright piano for the juke box to go quiet. Rocking in her tight orange dress, she played along, husky voice singing, "I cried . . . for you. . ." until Lelia came with her drink.

"Thanks, Kiddo. Tell Chuck he's slow tonight."

Hazel sipped her bourbon, looking out over the smoky room. "Ever listen to those lyrics? Pure chit. Crying for what you want never changed anybody's luck. I found that out a long time ago. When you want something bad enough, you have to figure out how to get it, that's a fact, pure and simple."

Lelia moved to go but Hazel said, "Wait up. Chuck wants me to wise you up about this place. Sit a minute. You'll be hopping around enough tonight."

She sat on the bench, watching Hazel's red nails play over the yellowed keys. Hazel was always a coiled spring of a woman, Lelia realized, the bristling energy coming to her now in waves of Evening in Paris perfume.

"You're a damn cool-acting cat, Kiddo, but Uncle Chuck agrees we don't know if you're innocent as a lamb or just quiet as a clam. Your eyes look like you know a thing or two, even if you did show up from some white-washed lil' town."

Hazel did a wicked chord and went on, "These guys we got here tonight? The whole lot of them—primed for trouble. They figure they'll be fighting Japs in some stinking jungle soon. They're looking for something to brag about Monday morning back at Drew Field or MacDill base or the Don CeSar hospital. Even the baby-faced ones."

"I can handle it," Lelia said. She could let herself block out their energy, their thoughts—that ability was her secret, her gift or her curse. This job was necessary. Having a place to stay with Hazel and Chuck was necessary, to be this close to Hurricane House, so close she could look across the narrow bay and see the patch of jungle hiding it over there on the gulf. All the family secrets she came to find were in that house. Held by the strange woman recluse in that house. . . .

Grouper Hole
Sunday, May 6, 1945

"Sundays are different from Saturday nights in this place," Chuck had promised. "The sandy crowd shows up in a lazy stupor from too much beach sun."

By noon, they knew this Sunday would be anything but ordinary. By midday, the sunburned sandy crowd and the GIs and airmen were filling the smoky bar room. Under the throb of juke box beat, the small Philco behind the bar chattered with the news—the war in Europe was about to end.

Lelia raced from kitchen to bay porch to booths with plates of crab cakes and trays of pop. For the first time she enjoyed the energy of the place. Subdued energy as yet, but crackling with expectation.

Pink-nosed girls, their bathing suits rolled in wet towels, stood around the Wurlitzer, feeding in nickels, and drinking lemon Cokes. Diana Shore's voice flowed out, the yearning notes smooth as cream. *"You'd be soo nice to come home to. . . ."*

Wandering in, faces flushed with unaccustomed sun, were the balding men in their baggy shorts, their wives in sun dresses, here on this gulf coast to visit sons and daughters. They gazed around with half-smiles, taking in pine walls hung with nets and hats and mounted with hard shapes of dusty fish.

When Lelia brought their ten-cent sodas and the three-for-a quarter crab cakes, they held her with expectant faces, needing to talk.

"Look at this pretty girl here on this old waterfront." "Honey, have you ever seen Miami Beach? White gloved doormen down there on Miami Beach."

"Not like this west coast. But sleeping's fine in that dinky cottage we're staying in over at the beach, windows open to the sweetest breeze and sound of surf."

A portly fellow beamed up at Lelia, "Like I told the better-half just now. One of these days, I wouldn't mind just packing up and moving down here. Have an orange tree in the front yard. Let life be as simple as that. You could live longer down here in this old sleepy Florida. No worries, no heating bills, no traffic. . . ."

Two couples from Lansing had Lelia take their pictures. They stood close under Moby Flounder on the wall, beaming toward their Brownie camera, chorusing, "V-E Day" as the juke box wailed and Lelia snapped the picture.

At the bar, Chuck shouted, "Lelia, pull the plug on the juke." He turned up the bar radio to a vibrating squawk as Artie Shaw's clarinet went quiet. Murmurs faded as the crowd listened to the radio voice, solemn and triumphant:

"After five year, eight months and six days, the European warfare, greatest, bloodiest and costliest war in human history, is about to come to an end . . . General

Eisenhower is now in headquarters at Reims, France, to meet with the Chief of Staff of the German Army...."

A young Coast Guardsman sloshed a spiral of beer suds with his leap from the bar stool. "I'm going back to Kansas and marry Florrie Putnam. If she's not around, maybe Dottie Enholm."

"Forget Kansas, Sonny," a burly MP growled. "We gotta whip Hirohito's ass first. Why you think we're here, being inoculated by Florida mosquitoes? Getting ready for the Pacific where they're bigger'n hornets."

"Not funny, McGee."

Artie Shaw's clarinet resumed its wail.

AUG 2000

Northport - E. Northport Public Library
185 Larkfield Road
E. Northport, N. Y. 11731
261-2313